A TILLING NEW YEAR

A Tilling New Year – A story of Mapp & Lucia in the Style of the Originals by E.F.Benson
Hugh Ashton

ISBN-13: 978-1-912605-73-6

ISBN-10: 1-91-260573-2

Published by j-views Publishing, 2021

© 2021 Hugh Ashton & j-views Publishing

All rights reserved. Without limiting the rights under copyright reserved above, no part of this publication may be reproduced, stored in or introduced into a retrieval system, or transmitted, in any form, or by any means (electronic, mechanical, photocopying, recording, or otherwise) without the prior written permission of both the copyright owner and the above publisher of this book.

This is a work of fiction. Names, characters, places, brands, media, and incidents are either the product of the author's imagination or are written in respectful tribute to the creator of the principal characters.

www.HughAshtonBooks.com

www.j-views.biz

publish@j-views.biz

j-views Publishing, 26 Lombard Street, Lichfield, WS13 6DR, UK

CONTENTS

INTRODUCTION	iv	NINETEEN	96
PROLOGUE	1	TWENTY	101
ONE	5	TWENTY-ONE	105
TWO	10	TWENTY-TWO	107
THREE	16	TWENTY-THREE	113
FOUR	20	TWENTY-FOUR	117
FIVE	27	TWENTY-FIVE	121
SIX	36	TWENTY-SIX	125
SEVEN	39	TWENTY-SEVEN	127
EIGHT	43	TWENTY-EIGHT	130
NINE	47	TWENTY-NINE	133
TEN	53	THIRTY	136
ELEVEN	59	THIRTY-ONE	141
TWELVE	63	THIRTY-TWO	144
THIRTEEN	67	THIRTY-THREE	148
FOURTEEN	72	THIRTY-FOUR	153
FIFTEEN	78	EPILOGUE	155
SIXTEEN	82	IF YOU ENJOYED THIS STORY	166
SEVENTEEN	87	ABOUT THE AUTHOR	168
EIGHTEEN	94		

INTRODUCTION

This is my fourth Mapp and Lucia pastiche in less than a year. I confess to having suffered some trepidation when I started writing these books in 2020.

Firstly, stepping into the shoes of another author is always a challenge. When the writer is so respected, and as astute with his observations and as much a master of language and obervation of his fellow human beings as 'Fred' Benson, this is a rather frightening prospect.

Secondly, there is the fear of rejection, by a highly knowledgeable body of experts on the inhabitants of Tilling – that is to say, the Mapp and Lucia group on Facebook. Much to my relief, their reactions have encouraged me to hope that there will be a market for this, my fourth such book.

The third reservation is very much a child of its time. All these books have been written in the midst of the COVID-19 pandemic, possibly the most serious, at least in its social consequences, such event to hit the world in the past few hundred years (the Black Death of the fourteenth century may well have killed a third of the European population and accelerated the death of the feudal system and the urbanisation of Europe, but it doesn't really count as recent). Isn't it frivolous to write light social comedy at such a time of tragedy?

The answer to this last seems to be that it is not – I have received several comments that have encouraged me to continue writing these tales, telling me that they have helped make a dark time lighter for their readers.

So, here we are in Tilling once again, with Elizabeth Mapp and Major Benjy, Lucia and Georgie Pillson, dear Diva, quaint Irene, the Padre and Evie, and Algernon and Susan Wyse, as they dash from Twistevant's to Rice's to Hopkins', doing their marketing, and spreading news and rumours about each others' doings.

And what doings! Bridge, of course, is one of the leisure passions of this little group, but

Hugh Ashton – v

even the pleasures of bridge can pall after a while, and what more natural than that Mapp should discover an alternative to entertain her fellow-Tillingites? And, acting on the principle of an equal and opposite reaction, what more natural that Lucia should find a rival pastime to amuse the good people of Tilling?

Add the sudden appearance of Olga Bracely at Mallards, with a somewhat dishevelled and unusual companion in tow, and matters prove to be interesting.

My sincere thanks are due once again to Victoria Yardley who took on the task of spotting my mistakes, finding all the places where I had inadvertently used the wrong word or expression, or used the right one too often, or typed it wrongly. Not only did she carry out the task speedily, she also did it efficiently. The title of this book is also her suggestion. Any remaining infelicities are mine and mine alone.

Written in the hope that 2021 will see at least the start of the long climb out of the disaster that was 2020, and wishing all my readers a better and happy future.

Au reservoir!
Hugh Ashton, Lichfield, 2021

A TILLING NEW YEAR

A STORY OF MAPP & LUCIA IN THE STYLE OF THE ORIGINALS BY E.F. BENSON

HUGH ASHTON

{j} views

J-VIEWS PUBLISHING, LICHFIELD, UK

PROLOGUE

"And what is your resolution to be, Lucia?" asked Georgie, looking up from his petit point.

"My resolution? What on earth are you talking about?"

"It is New Year's Day in two days' time, and as the Padre reminded us on Sunday, it is the time to make a resolution for the New Year."

Lucia considered, her eyes fixed on some distant but yet invisible object. "I had not yet considered the matter. What is your resolution to be?"

"I had thought," Georgie told her, "that I should become a kinder person. But it's

PROLOGUE

sometimes hard to know exactly how one should go about such a matter."

"Especially when one's patience is tried so often," sighed Lucia.

There was a pause, during which both studiously avoided mentioning the name of Elizabeth Mapp-Flint.

The silence was broken by Grosvenor entering the room, bearing an envelope on a tray.

"Just arrived," she announced.

Lucia tore open the envelope and laughed. "One speaks of the devil," she announced. "From Grebe. 'Major and Mrs Mapp-Flint present the compliments of the season to Mr and Mrs Pillson, and request the pleasure of their company to welcome in the New Year. Nine o'clock, December 31. Black tie.' We're not busy that evening, are we?"

"Of course not," said Georgie. "No one is ever busy then. And I don't know why you mentioned speaking of the devil. We hadn't even mentioned her. And," he pulled himself up, "it won't do at all to be speaking of Elizabeth as the devil. Or even thinking of her in that way. If I'm going to keep this resolution of mine to be kind to everybody, I must not think horrid thoughts of them."

Lucia laughed her silvery laugh. "You sound

like dear Daisy's Guru in Riseholme. Do you remember?"

Georgie, who had never completely recovered from the loss of some of his most valued and loved bibelots, which had vanished together with the curry-cook who had instructed the inhabitants of Riseholme in Guru-ism, nodded. "All too well. But even if he was a curry-cook and not a real guru, the exercises that he taught us did do us all a lot of good, and he really did have the most noble and uplifting thoughts. We must take what is good from him," he finished, while ruminating sadly on all that was good that had been taken from him by the supposed Eastern spiritual master.

"Noble thoughts, *Georgino mio*," said Lucia. "You are right, we should seize this occasion of the New Year to improve ourselves. I must think carefully about how I may change my life for the better."

She crossed over to the desk and wrote a short note which she placed in an envelope before ringing for Grosvenor.

"Make sure this reaches Grebe before the end of today, if you please. Now," turning to Georgie, "what shall we wear?"

"I think you should wear the peacock-blue

Prologue

silk dress, with the Beethoven brooch. That is, if it is not too cold. Otherwise..."

"The peach satin?"

"Maybe." Georgie sounded a little dubious.

"Oo not like peach satin?"

"I like it well enough," Georgie answered. "But the waist has a tendency to ride up at times in a rather unbecoming fashion."

"Maybe you are right," Lucia said. "And you?"

"Well, it may be a bit daring, but I thought I might wear the electric blue cummerbund and bow-tie that you gave me for Christmas, together with my sapphire ring. I know that the invitation says 'black tie', but a little bit of festive colour would do no harm, I feel."

"And your outfit and mine, were I to wear the peacock-blue, would go well together, would they not?"

Georgie did not bother to give the obvious answer to this question. "Will there be dancing?" he wondered aloud.

"Dancing? Elizabeth and Benjy? A ridiculous notion." Lucia was visibly stifling her laughter.

"Now, now," Georgie said, smiling. "Remember what we agreed about not thinking ill of others." Despite his words, it seemed that he, too, had discovered some source of secret amusement.

ONE

In Grebe, the Mapp-Flints were planning the details of their party.

"She is *not* going to play the piano," Elizabeth said with an air of finality. There was no need for her to elucidate who was meant by the pronoun. There was only one person in Tilling who could and would take over one's piano and use it to entertain one's guests with a slow emotional rendering of the first movement of Beethoven's 'Moonlight Sonata'.

"We must lock the lid and lose the key," she went on. "I want our guests to enjoy themselves, not to suffer that interminable tune for the thousandth time."

ONE

"Quite right, Liz," replied her husband. "How many bottles shall we order?"

"Bottles of what?" asked Elizabeth, acutely aware of the circumstances that had attended her last social gathering, at which Benjy-boy had over-refreshed himself with disastrous results.

"Why, wine, whisky, lager beer, and so on."

"I hardly think that lager beer is in order, especially on a cold winter night. I think we shall have a hot punch, and a single bottle of red wine, together with some lemons, some suitable spices from the kitchen and hot water to taste will be sufficient to create it."

"Whisky, though, Liz," protested the Major. "An essential part of the celebration of Hogmanay, as they say north of the Border. For the Padre, if for no one else."

"Oh, very well," Elizabeth gave in. "But I warn you, Benjamin Mapp-Flint, if I discover that you have been over-indulging in whisky, it's the back bedroom for you for a month or more."

Benjy, who had unhappy memories of the lumpy mattress and chilly draughts that constituted the principal features of the back bedroom, nodded in assent. "And is there anything else that I should order when I am in town?" he asked. "Some lobster, perhaps? Good eating, I call it, that dish that Mrs Pillson brought with her from Riseholme."

Elizabeth who had less than fond memories of the infamous dish introduced to Tilling by Lucia, shuddered. Firstly, she had inadvisedly attempted to "borrow" the recipe for lobster *à la Riseholme*, and as a result of being in the wrong place at the wrong time had found herself marooned on an Italian trawler for several months. That in itself would have been bad enough, but the enforced confinement with Lucia had added a piquant twist of misery to the sea-sick Elizabeth's plight.

The notorious recipe, salt-stained and tattered, and starting with the mystic words "take two hen lobsters", had survived the adventures that it had shared with its possessor, and had been used to provide the crowning glory of a dinner-party to celebrate the engagement of Major Benjamin Flint and Miss Elizabeth Mapp. However, this had failed to produce the expected effect and cries of admiration, for Lucia, with the stealth and venom for which she was (in Elizabeth's eyes, anyway) infamous, had publicly accused her hostess (Elizabeth) of stealing the recipe from her (Lucia's) kitchen. The fact that she had not made the accusation in so many words, but had rather alluded

ONE

to it in vague but yet unmistakable terms, and, worst of all, the fact that the accusation was based on truth, compounded rather than mitigated the offence.

Since that day, the recipe for lobster à la Riseholme had languished unused at the bottom of Cook's recipe box.

"No, no lobster, thank you," she said firmly. "Far too rich and indigestible for poor Diva, you know, and I believe poor little Evie has an allergy to shellfish of all kinds. You may ask Mr Hopkins to send up a nice piece of cheap-cut salmon. Nothing so good as a nice piece of cold poached salmon after all the rich food over Christmas."

"How many people will be coming?"

"I have sent out invitations to eight, and I do not expect any refusals. That is to say, the Wyses, Diva, quaint Irene, the Padre and Evie, and Georgie and Lucia Pillson. With us, that will be ten. So you had better ask Hopkins for salmon to serve eight."

"I don't understand," Benjy replied. "If there will be ten of us, why are you asking for portions for eight?"

She sighed. "Hopkins always tries to sell one such wastefully large pieces of fish. His idea of fish for eight will easily feed ten."

8 – A Tilling New Year

"Oh, very well."

"And you may see in the baker's whether they have any of those little chocolate cakes of which Diva is so fond."

TWO

The next morning saw Lucia and Georgie sitting over breakfast as Grosvenor brought in the morning post.

Georgie opened an envelope addressed to him, and exclaimed as he read the contents. "How splendid!" he said to Lucia, who seemed to be engaged in the study of a seed catalogue.

"Yes, these wallflowers would look good along the south wall in the *giardino segreto*," she murmured to herself. "Oh," affecting to have noticed Georgie's comment for the first time. "You had something to say?"

"Yes, it's Olga."

He had no need to expand the name. Olga Bracely was an internationally renowned prima-donna who had arrived in Riseholme with her husband (now sadly deceased) some years previously and had captured the hearts of all the residents, with the possible exception of Lucia. Georgie had been particularly smitten by her kindness and her beauty, and indeed, he may be said to have fallen in love with her, married though she was, albeit his devotion to her was of the most perfectly chaste and honourable kind.

For her part, Lucia had been somewhat 'put out' by her temporary dethronement and the partial defection of her most devoted courtier, and had only fully recovered when Olga had undertaken a world tour, and Georgie was left behind in Riseholme.

For the brief period that Lucia and Pepino (her late husband) had lived in London, Olga had been a near neighbour in Brompton Square, and Lucia had applauded her fellow Riseholmeite enthusiastically in her title role of Lucrezia Borgia in the *première* of Cortese's opera of the same name.

Since then, there had been relatively few times when Olga's path and that of Lucia and Georgie had crossed, though Georgie had spent time in Le Touquet as a guest of Olga's, forming part of a larger house-party, including the

Two

Duchess of Sheffield ("dear Poppy", as Lucia was wont to refer to her), which had caused certain Tilling tongues to wag.

"Ah yes, the prima-donna," Lucia said absently. "We received a Christmas greetings-card from her, did we not?"

"Yes, yes, we did," replied Georgie. "But it's all too wonderful. She's coming to Tilling, and wonders if she could stay with us for a few days."

Lucia considered. She balanced the prestige of having an international *artiste* under her roof against the possibility (albeit a remote one) of Georgie falling prey to Olga's charms. Prestige won.

"It would be a pleasure to have her as a guest."

"She mentions a friend with whom she is travelling and wonders if the friend could also be accommodated," added Georgie, who had read a little further down the letter.

"There is a room in the attic which Major Benjy used when he and Elizabeth were flooded out of Grebe," Lucia said. "Olga can have the best spare room, and the friend, whoever she or he may turn out to be, may have the attic. When will she arrive?"

"New Year's Day, she says." He read from the letter. "'I hope you won't mind the terrible imposition, but the boat from Boulogne arrives in Dover on the afternoon of the 31st, and we will spend the night there before making our way to your beautiful Tilling the next day. Please telegraph to the following address' – it's a hotel in Biarritz – 'and let us know. With love to you and Lucia, Olga.' There. Isn't that a wonderful way to start the year?"

"It will be most pleasant," Lucia agreed. "We should certainly entertain some of our friends here so that they may meet her. The Padre and Evie, certainly. Perhaps he may be able to persuade Miss Bracely to sing at divine service on Sunday. The Wyses, of course – Mr Wyse is definitely of a type who will appreciate the culture that Miss Bracely will bring to Tilling. Irene, perhaps, so that she may see that being a great artist does not necessarily mean that one must divorce oneself from society's norms, and Diva to accompany her."

There were two names which were conspicuous by their absence, and Georgie questioned Lucia about them.

"We shall see," Lucia told him. "Poor Major Benjy's idea of music is hardly up to the standard that Miss Bracely will exhibit. Elizabeth, too. I fear that her tastes are not of the most exalted class. I still recall with horror that

Two

piano that stood here when I first rented this house from her."

"Oh yes," laughed Georgie. "Grandmamma Mapp's famous Blumenfelt. You soon put paid to that monstrosity, did you not? And how cross Elizabeth was when she discovered what you had done with her precious family heirloom."

"Even so," Lucia mused, "it would be a kindness to invite them."

"And it might cause friction if you do not," Georgie pointed out.

"That would never do," agreed Lucia. "My aim is always for sweet harmony to reign."

Georgie, who knew well that Lucia's idea of "sweet harmony" consisted chiefly of her having her own way regardless of others' opinions or wishes, held his peace on the matter. Rather than replying, he simply said, "Well, that's settled, then. I shall write and tell her that she is most welcome. And her friend too. I wonder how I can ask who the friend is without sounding too inquisitive."

"Shall we leave it as a surprise?"

"I think we will have to," Georgie sounded resigned to the idea. "Oh, Olga can be so secretive sometimes. It *is* tarsome." He wrote a few lines. "There, I'll go to the Post Office myself and send it off."

Two

Georgie rose and put on his scarf, coat, and hat. "It *will* be nice to see Olga again," he said. "She's sure to have lots of interesting news to tell us."

THREE

At Grebe, preparations continued for the New Year's Eve party. Hopkins had delivered salmon, but to Elizabeth's disappointment, had failed to display his usual over-generosity in the matter of portions. Looking at the orange slabs of fish, scarcely more than scraps, Elizabeth felt that they hardly constituted sufficient food for eight, let alone ten. For her and Benjy to go without was a possibility, to be sure, but not one which appealed.

If, however, the salmon were to be flaked and then mixed with breadcrumbs, a little butter and cream cheese, and delicately flavoured with red pepper, she was sure that a delicious *pâté* could be created, which could be served with economical rounds of toast and which would elegantly disguise the paucity of the principal ingredient.

She consulted Cook, who agreed that this was a possible solution to the problem, and even suggested that she might have a recipe somewhere which had been bequeathed to her by her mother, and which would fit the needs of the party admirably.

She had put the entertainment of the guests in Benjy's charge. He had originally suggested dancing Highland reels, but Elizabeth had put her foot down firmly.

"For one thing, we would have to take up the carpet, which would mean moving all the furniture, and where would we put it all, quite apart from the work it would involve? Then there is the question of music. We have agreed that the piano shall remain untouched throughout the evening, have we not?"

"We have a gramophone," he pointed out.

"And do we have any recordings of Scottish tunes? And where are we to find such at short notice?" Elizabeth countered. It was true that the Mapp-Flints' musical tastes did not run to such tunes, being more directed towards music-hall ditties of thirty years ago in Major

THREE

Benjy's case, or popular sentimental songs in the case of Elizabeth.

"And lastly," she concluded, "I have no knowledge of how to perform such a dance, and I very much doubt if you do, either."

"Easiest thing in the world, Liz," Benjy helpfully explained. "In India, all of us in the Mess used to knock back a few chota pegs, line up, and away we'd go." He hopped unsteadily from foot to foot, presumably in an attempt to demonstrate the steps needed to perform a reel.

"I am not going to 'knock back a few chota pegs', as you put it," Elizabeth retorted. "Neither are our guests. And you most certainly are not to do so. No, dancing of any kind, Scottish, English, French, or even Indian or Chinese is definitely not to form any part of the evening's programme. You must think of something else."

Benjy went away scratching his head. "I'll come up with something, Liz," he assured his wife.

Then there was the question of decorations. Of course, Elizabeth was well aware of the custom that Christmas decorations should remain in place until Twelfth Night, but the Christmas cards that she had received were all from the sixpenny or shilling trays, while she and Benjy had restricted their choices to the threepenny tray. In her opinion, it would be embarrassing for the senders of the sixpenny cards to see their poor offerings beside the more opulent and spectacular shilling greetings. They should all come down, she decided.

There was no question regarding the removal of the other Christmas decorations, since she and Benjy had not adorned the house, other than by tucking a few sprigs of holly behind the pictures hanging on the walls.

By two o'clock in the afternoon, the drawing-room had been cleaned and tidied to Elizabeth's satisfaction, and Benjy banned from there until the time the guests should arrive. On visiting the kitchen, Elizabeth professed herself to be pleased with the progress that had been made.

The evening promised to be one that all Tilling would remember, she thought to herself with a glow of satisfaction.

FOUR

Meanwhile in Mallards, Georgie and Lucia were busy preparing for the evening ahead. Foljambe had laid out Georgie's dinner suit and dress shirt, after carefully cleaning and pressing them, together with the cummerbund and bow-tie that he had daringly chosen to wear for the evening.

Lucia was luxuriating in her bath when the front doorbell rang.

"Oh bother," said Georgie crossly. "How tarsome. I hope that it's no one important," and continued to examine his cummerbund to ensure its emerald perfection remained untarnished.

There was a knock at the door. "Excuse me,

20 – A Tilling New Year

FOUR

sir," came Foljambe's voice, "but Miss Olga's here."

"Good heavens!" exclaimed Georgie. "Please make her comfortable and let her know that I will be with her in a few minutes."

"Very good, sir."

Georgie hurriedly adjusted his jacket, thankful that he had not yet begun changing for the party. On his way to the stairs he knocked on the bathroom door.

"Yes? What is it?" asked Lucia from her bath.

"Olga's just arrived. I'm going downstairs to meet her."

He made his way downstairs, happy to meet Olga, but as always, conscious of his feelings for her – feelings which he hardly dared to admit to himself, let alone to Olga.

"They're in the garden-room, sir," Foljambe told him as he reached the bottom of the stairs. "I will be bringing tea and cake to them as soon as they are ready."

"Oh, very good, Foljambe. Thank you so much." Taking a deep breath, he entered the garden-room, to be greeted by Olga's beautiful smiling face.

"Georgie!" she trilled. "I am so sorry that we are here so early, but all the hotels in Dover seemed either to be hideous beyond description, or all full up with no rooms available, so we came on here. I hope you don't mind."

"Not at all. Delighted to see you, but I'm afraid I don't think your rooms are quite ready," said Georgie. Conscious of the fact that he had just used the plural, Georgie noticed Olga's companion for the first time, somewhat shorter than either Olga or Georgie, clad in rather shabby garments with a vaguely foreign air to them, and with a shock of dark hair surmounting a face framed in a bushy beard.

"Oh, Georgie, meet Sasha," said Olga. "I am sorry, this is Alexander Davidovich Abramov. Sasha, this is Georgie."

"You call me Sasha, please," said the Russian (for so Georgie assumed him to be). He bowed and extended a small, rather dirty, hand, which Georgie took.

"Thank you, Sasha," said Georgie. "Welcome to Tilling."

Olga continued, "Sasha has fled from Russia—"

"Bolshevik pigs!" Sasha fairly spat out.

"Ssh, Sasha," Olga told him. "He is one of Russia's greatest composers," she explained to Georgie, "if not one of the greatest producers of opera in the whole world. We met in Paris, where I was singing Violetta, and he was in the audience. He is now writing his masterwork, *Tsarina Ekaterina*, and, lucky me, I am to sing Ekaterina when it is finished and performed for the first time."

"Well, that does sound exciting," said Georgie. "Oh, do sit down," he said as Foljambe brought in the tea things and started serving. "Foljambe, Miss Bracely and Mr Sasha here were going to arrive tomorrow, but they are here now."

"Yes, sir."

"So can you please make up their rooms for tonight?"

"Certainly, sir. Very pleased to see you again, madam," she said to Olga. Foljambe approved of Olga, since she always made Georgie so happy whenever they met, and treated Foljambe with perfect courtesy.

"Thank you, Foljambe," smiled Olga. To Georgie, she said, "Are you sure that we can stay tonight? I seem to remember there's quite a decent hotel here in Tilling."

"Not at all," he answered her. It will be a positive pleasure to have you here. Only..."

"There is problem?" Sasha asked.

"No, no, not at all. Just that the Mapp-Flints are having a party to mark New Year's Eve, and Lucia and I are invited."

Hugh Ashton – 23

FOUR

"Well, if you're sure you want Sasha and me to stay here—"

"Quite sure. But you must come with us to the Mapp-Flints. To be honest with you, we do see quite enough of each other in Tilling. Some fresh blood will do us good."

"No blood," said Sasha. "Too much blood in Russia. Bolshevik pigs," he repeated.

"No, Sasha," said Olga, and explained something to Sasha in a language that Georgie failed to understand. "German," she said to Georgie. "Sasha's English is not fluent, though I must say that he is improving, and my Russian is no better, so we must speak in German sometimes. Anyway, it is so sweet of you and Lucia to take care of us like this." She paused. "Lucia is well? You haven't murdered her and buried her in the garden or anything like that, have you?"

"Not at all," said Georgie indignantly. "She was taking a bath when you arrived, that's all. I'm sure she will be joining us shortly."

"Now, my dear, no need to be so cross about it. I was only joking. But how are you? How is Georgie? How is Lucia? Any news?" Olga asked greedily, quite in the spirit of Riseholme.

"Well, a rather amusing thing about Diva Plaistow. You remember her?"

"The lady who makes those funny little sardine tartlets? Yes, I remember her – and them – very well."

"Well, she had a new recipe for coffee cake, and she made some and she asked me to taste it. And it tasted horrible."

"Let me guess? She'd used salt instead of sugar?"

"You're nearly right. She'd used gravy browning powder instead of coffee. You see, she thought she'd be clever and save a lot of time and energy by using that new instant coffee. But she didn't."

"Oh, that is priceless," Olga laughed. "I thought that sort of thing only happened in Riseholme, but it seems it happens here as well. It must be your influence, Georgie."

At that moment, Lucia entered, wearing the dress that she planned to wear to the party. Sasha and Olga rose.

"Dear Olga," Lucia exclaimed. "What a pleasure to have you here."

Olga explained once again about the hotels in Dover, and introduced Lucia to Sasha, who crossed the room, bowing low over Lucia's hand, which he kissed rather too loudly, much to Lucia's embarrassment.

Georgie explained that the rooms for Olga

FOUR

and Sasha were being prepared, and Lucia took her usual seat by the window, accepting a cup of tea and a plate of cake from Georgie.

"And you will come to Elizabeth and Benjy's party, won't you?" she asked.

"If you are sure we will be welcome."

"Dear Olga, how could you possibly not be welcome anywhere you go? And you, too, Mr. Abramov."

"Sasha, please, Mrs. Lucia," he answered.

"What time are we expected?" Olga asked.

"Nine o'clock is the time on the invitations."

"Then there will be time to get out of these old things," Olga gestured at her smart travelling-dress, "and make myself presentable. You too, Sasha," she said, adding something in German.

"Very well," said Lucia. "Let us finish our tea, and I will show you to your rooms."

FIVE

A little before nine, the party set out from Mallards, Cadman at the wheel of Lucia's car. Lucia and Georgie were in their best Hitum outfits, and Olga was arrayed in an elegant dress which had the mark of Paris all over it, making it, in its simplicity of style, more Hitum than Hitum. Sasha was dressed in a tailcoat, albeit one which had clearly seen better days, and his hair and beard were in a much tidier state than when Georgie had first beheld them.

Withers admitted the little party to Grebe, and led them to the drawing-room where Elizabeth and Benjy received them. It appeared that they were the first to arrive.

"Dear Elizabeth," Lucia smiled. "We have had

FIVE

such a delightful surprise. Our dear friend Olga Bracely – the prima-donna, you know – and the famous Russian composer Mr Abramov were due to come and stay with us tomorrow, but circumstances meant that they were forced to arrive today. I do apologise for swelling the numbers, but I thought it was so important that they should not spend New Year's Eve alone, and that they should take advantage of such a marvellous opportunity to meet the whole of Tilling society in such magnificent surroundings." She waved a negligent hand in the general direction of the Mapp-Flints' sparsely furnished drawing-room.

"You know, dear Lulu, that you and your guests, no matter how many they may be, or where they may be from, are always welcome," smiled Elizabeth, displaying her splendid teeth. The Biblical story of loaves and fishes came to her mind, as she wondered whether the toast and salmon *pâté* would prove sufficient to feed the extra mouths that Lucia had so thoughtlessly added to the party. Nonetheless, she managed to greet Olga and Sasha with what she trusted was sufficient cordiality and passed them on to her husband.

Major Benjy, clearly impressed by Olga's magnificence, personally escorted the Mallards party to the table on which stood glasses and a jug of aromatic punch.

"I'll leave you to do the honours, old man," he said to Georgie. "I see the Padre and his little woman have just arrived."

Georgie ladled some of the punch into four glasses, taking great care not to spill any on his best clothes.

"A very happy New Year to you, Elizabeth," he called across the room, raising his glass in her direction. "And to you, Major."

The toast was echoed by the other three of the Mallards party, as the Padre and Evie crossed to join them and Georgie poured out two more glasses of the tepid liquid.

"And may I wish ye all a very mirthful Hogmanay," said the Padre. "'Tis a bonny sight to behold ye again, Mistress Bracely."

Olga, who had encountered the Padre on a previous visit to Tilling, seemed to be at home with his mixture of Scottish and medieval speech, but Sasha, who was sipping mournfully at his punch, appeared to be completely nonplussed by these words. He muttered something, presumably in German, to Olga, who replied in the same language.

Major Benjy came over to them and detached Georgie from the rest of the party.

Hugh Ashton – 29

FIVE

"I say, Pillson, old man. That Russkie with you. Know him?"

"Not really, no," confessed Georgie. "But he's a friend of Miss Bracely's, and I've known her for many years."

"Fine figure of a woman," commented the Major. "Lucky you to have such friends. But this Russian... He's not a Bolshie, is he?"

"I believe that he has fled Russia to escape the Bolsheviks, if I understand him rightly. He's a very famous composer, so Miss Bracely tells me."

"On our side, eh? That's a relief, I must say. How do you address him? Sasha. Excellent. Sasha," he called to the Russian. "Please join us. Georgie Pillson tells us you are on our side."

"I sorry. I do not understand."

"You do not like the Bolsheviks," Georgie elaborated.

"I hate them. I spit on them, and their mothers and fathers, and the graves of their mothers and fathers," Sasha said angrily. "My *Rodina* – my Motherland – she is in the hands of animals." He took a gulp of the punch, and shuddered. "This drink. What is in it?" he asked Benjy.

"Wine, water, some cinnamon and ginger, I believe."

"Is weak. Needs strength. See." From a pocket of his tailcoat, Sasha produced a small silver hip flask and poured a colourless liquid from it into his glass. "Vodka," he explained. "We can buy in Paris, perhaps not here in England. You try?" he asked Benjy.

"Why, certainly. I may as well live dangerously, eh, Pillson? That is to say, more dangerously than usual," with a meaning glance at Elizabeth, now engaged in greeting Algernon and Susan Wise. "We married men know all about living dangerously, don't we?" He nudged Georgie in the ribs with his elbow.

"Oh yes. Quite so, quite so," Georgie replied meekly.

"For you?" Sasha offered, holding the flask above Georgie's glass.

"No, no, thank you."

"Good. Is more for me and my friend here," Sasha answered him. "*Za vas*," he said. "To you," he toasted, raising his half-full glass and downing the contents in a gulp.

"*Quai hai*," replied the Major, and Georgie offered a timid "Your health," before sipping politely at his drink, but Benjy followed Sasha's lead and emptied his glass heroically. Immediately he started coughing violently, his face turning bright red with the exertion.

Hugh Ashton –

FIVE

"Benjy-boy," Elizabeth called from the door. "You must greet dear Susan and Algernon. Come here. What has happened."

"Crumb ... went ... down ... the ... wrong ... way," explained the Major through bouts of coughing.

Elizabeth, who was fully conscious of the fact that the food for the gathering had yet to be set out, and that crumbs were therefore unlikely to be the cause of the Major's distress, forbore to press the matter further, but allowed her husband to splutter his way through his greetings to the new arrivals without making any comment.

Georgie and Sasha moved to rejoin Lucia, Olga and the Bartletts. It appeared that Lucia was holding forth on the subject of music, to which Olga appeared to be listening with rapt attention.

"...and that final noblest passage of the symphony is why, in my humble and uninformed opinion, Beethoven is the greatest of all musical geniuses of any age. Do you not agree, Miss Bracely?"

"Undoubtedly," Olga replied, but to Georgie's experienced eye, there was a slight note of humour in her voice, which seemed to pass unnoticed by Lucia.

Sasha, however, held out in his broken English for Mozart as the greatest composer.

"Ah, *divino Mozartino*," said Lucia. "Such joy to play his greatest pieces arranged for four hands on the piano, is it not, Georgie?"

"Oh, indeed it is," Georgie hurriedly agreed. At that moment, the Wyses joined the little group, and Georgie, who seemed to have been pressed into the *rôle* of bartender, hastened to fill their glasses, as well as that of Sasha, who presented his empty glass to Georgie expectantly.

The door opened, and Irene Coles and Diva Plaistow, who, as the whole of Tilling knew, either directly or indirectly by way of Diva's maid Janet, had arranged to share a taxi from Tilling to Grebe, entered the room.

"What ho, all!" called Irene in a voice which would have carried across the Channel, displaying those qualities which Elizabeth had remarked as 'quaint'. "And a jolly fine Hogmanay to all and sundry."

Georgie had been looking in Sasha's direction as the two latest arrivals entered, and was struck by the change in his expression.

"Is not possible," Sasha murmured to himself. His face was a deathly white, and he stared

FIVE

wide-eyed in Diva's direction. "Not possible," he whispered to himself.

"What is it, Sasha?" asked Olga, who had also noticed the change in his mood and expression.

By way of answer, she was treated to a long diatribe in German, which only she appeared to understand. At the end of this speech, Sasha sank, seemingly overcome by emotion, into a convenient chair, and pulled out his hip flask from which he took a drink.

The whole company had by now arranged themselves around Sasha, and when he had finished speaking, Olga turned to the others. "He says," she reported, "that Mrs Plaistow here is the living image of his late wife, who died five years ago. In fact, he was convinced that he had seen his wife's ghost just now."

"Who is he, anyway?" asked Irene in her usual direct fashion, while accepting a glass of punch held out to her by Georgie.

Olga explained.

"Oh, *that* Abramov," answered Irene, clearly impressed. "I remember seeing a production of his *Baba Yaga* in London once. Wild music." She paused. "Didn't like the scenery, though."

"Could you have done better, do you think?" Olga asked her. "I'm not trying to be rude. It's a serious question."

"Then I'll answer it seriously," Irene said. For all her disdain for most of the human race, Irene had a genuine respect for Olga, who had achieved her success through her ability and hard work, and her art. "Yes, I could do better."

"How would you like to be responsible for the scenery and costumes for his new opera, *Tsarina Ekaterina*?"

"I'd have to be away from our dear Tilling, and I'd miss you, Mapp, and Major Benjy-Wenjy, and you, dear Lucia, and my sweet Georgie, and all the rest of you, wouldn't I? But yes, oh yes, what an adventure it would be."

"I'll talk to Sasha about it," Olga promised.

Meanwhile, the composer of *Tsarina Ekaterina* was sitting open-mouthed and staring at Diva, the hip-flask still clutched in his hand.

SIX

The scene was rapidly becoming an embarrassing one, with Diva seemingly deeply disturbed by Sasha Abramov's identification of her with his deceased wife.

Though Diva's discomfiture was not a wholly unpleasing sight to Elizabeth, she nonetheless had the wit to realise that the recall of Sasha's memories was a scene of some distress to other guests, and gave orders to Withers to bring in the food that had been prepared in the kitchen. Her orders to her husband were to remove Sasha to a place where he would not embarrass the other guests.

"You may take him to your study, if you wish, and tell him about your Indian tigers."

"Why would he be interested in those, Liz?" Benjy asked, puzzled by the request.

"He's as likely to be interested in them as he is in anything else," she answered. "You must take his mind off his wretched wife."

If the truth be told, Benjy was only too glad to escape to another room in the company of the Russian – and, more importantly, of his hip-flask which contained that surprisingly powerful liquid which he had named as 'vodka'. The Major had a sneaking suspicion that a mixture of this new liquor and whisky would not go amiss.

It took a little persuasion to move Sasha from the chair into which he had collapsed, but eventually he permitted himself to be guided into the Major's study, where he sat in the comfortable wing chair facing Benjy, and gratefully accepted a glass of whisky from the bottle that was kept in a secret drawer in the desk, of which Elizabeth dutifully pretended that she had no knowledge.

"Drink up, old man," the Major said in a reassuring voice as he lifted his own glass in salute. "Plenty more fish in the sea. Mrs Plaistow, well, she's a fine woman, but..." He took a sip of his drink and sighed. "I remember once in India. This saucy little baggage we used to call

Six

the Pride of Poona. I looked at her, but did she ever look at me? I tell you, sir, she did not. Hey," breaking off, "I see your glass is as empty as mine..."

SEVEN

Meanwhile, in the drawing-room, the guests were partaking of, if not actually enjoying, the fruits of the labours undertaken earlier in Elizabeth's kitchen. The salmon *pâté* was generally judged to be somewhat subtle in taste, the subtlety perhaps enhanced by the proportion of breadcrumbs to salmon.

Olga busied herself in explaining to Diva that Sasha had always professed himself to be devoted to his late wife, and that far from its being an insult, Diva should regard it as a high compliment to be taken as the double of the wife of the greatest living composer of opera.

Elizabeth, painfully aware that the attention of the party was not on her, moved among her

SEVEN

guests, with a jug of weak punch, and an even weaker smile, but it was painfully clear that the chief object of interest of those assembled was in the other room with her husband.

There was a lull in the conversation, and from outside the room came an extraordinary noise.

"It is a walrus!" exclaimed the Padre, forgetting to be either Scotch or medieval. "It is a sound I well remember from the time when I was taken to the Zoological Gardens in Regents Park as a child."

"A walrus in Tilling! How exciting!" exclaimed Susan Wyse.

"How could it possibly have got here?" asked Lucia. "We must tell the police."

Mr Wyse bowed slightly to them all. "If I may make a suggestion, Mrs Pillson, I do not think that the police will have sufficient experience to deal with such a strange occurrence. It might, I venture, be more profitable to establish contact with the Zoo at Brighton."

"Or perhaps the Museum or the Town Hall?" squeaked Evie.

"We should not let the poor creature go unaided. Listen, it seems to be in some distress."

All dutifully listened, and indeed, the sounds certainly seemed to indicate some degree of discomfort.

"May we use your telephone, dear Elizabeth?" asked Lucia.

"You may do so, but I do not think that anyone will be answering the telephone at half-past ten on New Year's Eve."

Elizabeth's remark left the company a little bereft of words. It was certainly true that there would be no one available to deal with a walrus at this time of night, New Year or not.

Georgie looked at Olga, who appeared to be in the grip of some powerful emotion. Her pretty face was contorted, and her shoulders were heaving.

Irene burst into peals of laughter. "Oh, you are all such fools. That, my dear fellow revellers, seems to me to be the aria sung by the hero in Abramov's opera *Baba Yaga*. Though I have to say it is being performed extraordinarily badly, if my memory of the performance that I saw is correct."

They all looked at each other in astonishment.

Olga composed herself, and explained, "Irene is quite correct. It is a song of lament as the singer mourns his lost love. You are now hearing it, I believe, sung by the composer himself. He possesses an extraordinarily powerful bass voice, which could have made his fortune as a performer, had he been able to hold a tune.

Seven

Unfortunately, that is not the case, but even so, Miss Coles has been able to identify the piece he was attempting to sing."

There was a stunned silence, broken by Elizabeth. "So glad it has been cleared up. How foolish of you, Padre, and you Lucia and Diva, to imagine that it was a walrus. Of all things, a walrus in Tilling!" She laughed, a little less than pleasantly. "So no need for a telephone call after all. More punch, anyone? Another chocolate cake, Diva?"

Georgie was relieved that he had not taken part in the discussion regarding the supposed sea-beast, as he watched the shamefaced reactions of the others. It was rather amusing, though, if he were honest with himself, to see the confusion on their faces.

Olga, clearly recognising that her explanation had caused embarrassment, chose to change the subject. "May we romp a little, Mrs Mapp-Flint? Do you know how to play Clumps?"

Before long, the group was divided into two, with each group in turn attempting to guess the object that had been thought of by the other, and the walrus had been almost forgotten, except by Elizabeth, who was unable to remain unconcerned as to the fate of the companion of the 'walrus'.

EIGHT

Under Olga's skilful direction, the evening passed pleasantly and quickly enough. Diva's embarrassment at being taken for a deceased Russian wife of uncertain vintage passed, and she joined in the games and amusements led by Olga.

Despite Lucia's hints to Elizabeth that Olga be allowed to delight the company with her singing (presumably to be followed by further such musical delights, namely the first movement of the 'Moonlight Sonata' to be performed on the piano by Lucia, followed by a series of interminable duets by her and Georgie), Elizabeth held out against such pressures, directing Lucia to a thin slice of seed-cake or another

EIGHT

glass of equally thin punch, and simply refusing to acknowledge the less than subtle hints that were thrown in her direction.

The sound of the 'walrus' had ceased at some point in the evening, but had been replaced by the sound of what sounded like, but almost certainly was not, the sound of a growling tiger. Elizabeth recognised it immediately, however, as the sound of her husband's snoring, but refrained from informing the company, who had a shrewd idea of its source, but tactfully refrained from passing comment on it.

At length midnight was upon them, bringing in the New Year, but it appeared that no one was interested in joining hands and singing 'Auld Lang Syne', and contenting themselves with perfunctory greetings and good wishes for the coming year, the guests started to depart. The Mallards party prepared to leave, but suddenly Olga gave out a little cry.

"Sasha! Where is Sasha?"

In the excitement of the romps that Olga had organised, both Georgie and Lucia had completely forgotten the Russian's existence.

"Elizabeth, dear," smiled Lucia. "May I just pop into the other room and find my houseguest? I do know the way. No need to trouble yourself on my account."

EIGHT

Elizabeth, who was well aware that Lucia knew every nook and cranny of Grebe as well as she did herself, and had no wish for her to come upon her husband in what she feared was a deplorable state, placed herself strategically in front of the door that led to Benjy's study in such a way that physical force would be needed to go past her.

"So sweet of you to consider me, dear Lulu," she smiled. "I will just go and find him myself, though. *Ce n'est pas trop pour moi.*"

She disappeared, and Olga, Lucia, and Georgie all looked at each other. Olga was clearly trying not to laugh as Elizabeth reappeared, a look of thunder on her face which rearranged itself into a mirthless smile as she approached her guests, and accompanied by an unsteady Sasha.

"Ah, dear Olga!" Sasha exclaimed, moving forwards towards her with his arms outstretched in what was obviously an attempt to enfold her in a bear-like hug. She sidestepped the advance neatly, and Sasha staggered forward into a cabinet on which stood a vase, which tottered perilously before falling into the hands of Georgie, who had foreseen the accident and moved swiftly to avert disaster.

"Oh, thank you, Mr Georgie," said Elizabeth,

EIGHT

who had been watching the action unfold with a horrified gaze in a state of seeming paralysis. "That was one of dear Aunt Caroline's favourite pieces, from the days when she lived in Mallards." She sighed. "I remember it so well from that time, and it always held a place of honour in the garden-room when I lived there."

Meanwhile, Olga had taken charge of Sasha, bundling him into his coat, and hustling him out of the door where he could do no further damage. Lucia hurried after them, leaving Georgie, vase in hand, to make his farewells on behalf of the rest of the party.

"Thank you, Elizabeth, for a very enjoyable evening," he stammered.

"A pleasure," she answered through clenched teeth. "Delighted. So pleased."

Georgie suddenly became acutely aware that he was holding Elizabeth's vase. "May I be permitted?" he asked, and replaced it on the place where it had formerly stood. "My compliments to Major Mapp-Flint," he added, but realised from the expression on Elizabeth's face that he had made something of a tactical error. "Er... goodnight, then," he half-gabbled, and beat a hasty retreat.

NINE

Elizabeth Mapp-Flint was under few illusions as to what she would find when she entered the study, and she was not disappointed in her expectations.

Her husband was sprawled in an armchair, an empty glass beside him, and he was snoring with that tiger-like roar that she had previously remarked. There was little or nothing to be gained by waking him, she considered, so she turned off the light and closed the door on him before taking herself to bed, locking the bedroom door behind her.

As she lay in bed, vainly attempting to sleep, angry thoughts swirled in her brain like storm clouds.

NINE

Firstly, her husband. How dare he, after all that had taken place in the past, drink himself into a stupor at a social gathering that had been so carefully planned and arranged?

And Lucia? How dare she bring two uninvited guests to her gathering, blithely assuming that there would be enough provided in the way of refreshments to accommodate them? Admittedly, having the world-famous prima-donna under her roof might have been regarded as a *coup de théâtre* had it been Elizabeth's own initiative that had brought it about, but an accidental *coup* such as this was almost worse than no *coup* at all.

Then Olga's 'grabby' (she could think of no better word) behaviour in monopolising her guests and directing the gathering in a direction which was not in the least what she had planned for them. The fact that it had been admirably executed only rubbed salt into the wound, since there was nothing to criticise in that direction.

And that nasty little Russian man. She had to laugh at the credulity of her fellow-Tillingites in believing that the sound they had heard was that of a walrus. To be fair to Benjy, she told herself, it might well have been the influence of the Russian, whose performance with the hip-flask she had observed, who could be held at least partly responsible for the state in which Major Benjamin Mapp-Flint now found himself. Famous composer though he might be (though she doubted the truth of that), he would never darken her doors again.

She managed to find some peace when considering Georgie's actions in saving her vase from destruction. She had to admit some degree of mitigation there, but oh! the mad bear-like charge of the crazed Russian! Surely that wiped out anything positive, and in any case Georgie was at least party to the introduction of the Russian Revolution to Grebe.

The major offenders had been tried and found guilty in the court of her mind, but awaited final sentencing. The lesser offenders were now brought up to the bench.

The Padre, of course. How absurd to set the whole party on the track of an imagined sea-beast! And little Evie, no better in her encouragement.

She had always considered Mr Wyse to be possessed of a fair degree of common sense, even if his manners were more than a little affected at times. But tonight... Oh dear... And foolish Susan, clearly thrilled to the core by the preposterous idea of a walrus in Tilling!

NINE

Quaint Irene. How coarse in her open appraisal of the others as "fools" (though of course Elizabeth might agree privately with this classification, she would never say so outright other than to herself). Furthermore, Elizabeth strongly suspected her of having celebrated New Year by imbibing some strong liquor prior to her arrival at Grebe.

And lastly, dear Diva. Old friend as she was, Elizabeth was certain that Diva's greed, especially for those little chocolate cakes, would prove her undoing. Five had vanished this evening by way of Diva's plate (Elizabeth had been keeping careful watch) and what might objectively be considered an excessive quantity of salmon *pâté* had taken the same route. Indeed, Elizabeth herself had had little chance to taste it, and of course, poor Benjy had had no food that evening.

The realisation of the fact that whatever her husband had drunk that evening had been on an empty stomach did not excuse his behaviour, but made him fractionally less culpable in his eyes. Of course, the Russian was behind it all.

Having settled the verdicts, and duly considered all mitigating circumstances, it was time to move to the most pleasurable part of the proceedings – passing sentence.

As birds of passage, the Russian and Olga might be given a relatively light punishment for their misdeeds. There would, naturally, be no subsequent welcome for them at Grebe, and, should an invitation arrive for Benjy and her to a musical evening at Mallards to feature Olga and that Russian, it would find them positively and incontrovertibly engaged for that time.

For the other Tillingites, the usual penalties would apply. Adherence to the strictest possible rules of bridge with regard to revoking, dealing etiquette, and so on, together with constructive obstructive deliberations while marketing, forcing others to wait, and a certain tardiness in replies to any invitations to teas, and so on.

But the greatest penalties of all should be reserved for Lucia, who by her dastardly actions in bringing the prima-donna and the Russian had once more managed to destroy Elizabeth's social ambitions.

It was hard to imagine just what would fit the bill, but there would be something appropriate. It would be appropriate if music were involved – some disaster occurring in the middle of one of Lucia and Georgie's innumerable and interminable duets. Or perhaps painting – it was a shame that Elizabeth had been forced to resign her position on the Hanging Committee of the Tilling Art Club, otherwise there were several kinds of mischief that could be worked there. Or the church and dear Padre might offer some possible openings... Then there was the Contessa Faradiddleony or whatever Mr Wyse's sister Amelia chose to call herself – Lucia had wiggled her way out of one trap that Elizabeth had believed to be foolproof when it came to her Italian language ability. But there would be other occasions.

With such pleasant thoughts running through her mind, Elizabeth drifted off to sleep. So soundly did she rest that she failed to hear her husband creeping up the stairs in his stockinged feet and stealthily turning the door-handle, only to discover a locked door, before he tiptoed downstairs to return to his armchair, rather than face the horrors of the back bedroom mattress once more.

TEN

Diva awoke the next morning a little later than usual, on account of the party the previous night. There was something at the back of her mind which was disturbing and unsettling her, and she found it difficult to remember what it was. She had a slight headache, but that, she reflected, would have nothing to do with anything she had drunk the previous evening – all Tilling knew that it was possible to drink large quantities of Elizabeth's fruit punch without suffering any effect, good or ill, that evening or the next day.

It suddenly came back to her that she was apparently the double of the deceased wife of that extraordinary Russian whom Lucia had

TEN

brought with her to the party the previous evening. It was, she supposed, flattering to be the object of such attention. In the taxi she had shared with Irene coming home, she had asked Irene more about the Russian, and she had been assured that he was indeed famous, not a Bolshevik, and as far as Irene was aware, unmarried since the death of his wife, whom he was generally considered to have loved deeply.

All this, she considered, was flattering rather than otherwise, but being adored by a Russian composer on account of her resemblance to his deceased wife was a turn of events that was not entirely welcome to her.

She went down to breakfast, to discover on her plate an envelope addressed to her in a handwriting she did not recognise. There was no stamp.

"Where did this come from, Janet?" she asked her maid.

"Don't know, I'm sure," came the reply. "It was on the mat this morning when I came down."

Diva sat down eagerly and attacked her eggs with gusto. Mysterious envelopes could wait, she told herself, but to neglect eggs scrambled to perfection by Janet and accompanied by crisp hot toast fingers would be an act akin to sacrilege.

The eggs having been disposed of, she poured herself a second cup of strong milky tea with three spoonfuls of sugar and slit open the envelope to extract a half-sheet of stiff paper with sprawling handwriting in deep black ink.

'Dear Mrs Plaistow,' she read. *'Mrs Lucas give me your name when I ask her. Please excuse behaviour of last night. I lose my wife some years in past, and your face and look is just as she had. Miss Olga also tell me that you have unfortunate loss of husband, so we in same ship, as you say in English.*

I will visit to talk to you this afternoon. Please to excuse impoverished English.

With affectionate regard

Alexander Davidovich Abramov'

Diva had to read this extraordinary missive twice more before the whole import sank in. So this Mr Abramov seemed to have a romantic interest in her, did he? This would have to end, but she was unsure if she was the person to accomplish the cutting of the strings. A third party would have to act as the go-between. Who to ask?

Of course, she would never dream of asking Elizabeth to act in this matter. Then there was quaint Irene, who would probably regard the whole business as screamingly amusing, and do nothing but laugh. That left Susan Wyse

Ten

as another possibility. No. Dear Susan might have a kind heart, but as Elizabeth had once so unkindly (if amusingly) remarked, dear Susan had been all too modest in coming forward when the dear Lord was giving out brains and had therefore failed to receive her fair share. A pity, Elizabeth had added, that Susan's sense of modesty had since deserted her.

Lucia, as Mr Abramov's hostess, should surely take some responsibility for her guest's actions, but there was the disadvantage that this would place Diva under a constant obligation to her – an obligation that would somehow require her always to take Lucia's part in the warfare that arose between Grebe and Mallards at irregular intervals, and this was a duty that she felt unwilling to take on. Much as she hated to admit it, there were times when Elizabeth was in the right and Lucia in the wrong, and it would go against her moral sense to knowingly take the wrong side.

Of course, another possibility was always Miss Bracely who know this Russian well, but Diva was shy of asking such a world-famous personality for a personal favour of this nature.

She paused in her thoughts, and absentmindedly stirred three teaspoons of sugar into her tea before taking a sip, and realising that she had already sweetened her tea. The resulting sickly mess was almost undrinkable, even to Diva, who was generally considered to be in possession of the sweetest tooth in Tilling. She continued her rumination, concentrating this time on her the men of her circle. Her feeling was that her unwanted suitor would be more likely to listen to a man than a woman.

Algernon Wyse was perhaps the most diplomatic of her male acquaintances, with the most *savoir-faire*, but she was sure that if she could summon up the courage to unburden herself to him with regard to this matter, she would be unable to look him in the face ever again. The same could be said of the Padre.

Major Benjamin Mapp-Flint she dismissed without a second thought.

Georgie Pillson had never struck her as being anything other than sympathetic, and, if she made due allowance for the fact that he was married to Lucia, straightforward and honest. Furthermore, she knew that Georgie enjoyed a close relationship with Olga Bracely (though she refused to follow Elizabeth's lead on the supposed precise closeness of the friendship) and it might therefore be possible to kill two birds with one stone. She was unsure of the appropriateness of the last metaphor to describe

TEN

the addition of two new recruits to her cause with one request, but she was unable to come up with a better one.

She rose from the table, and went to her bureau to write a short note to Georgie, requesting him to visit her at Wasters at half past ten, or as close to that time as was convenient, before putting it in an envelope and giving it to Janet to deliver.

Having done that, she busied herself with the rearrangement of her preserve cupboard until such time as he should arrive.

ELEVEN

Georgie Pillson arrived at the appointed time, resplendent in a smart suit with a fur-trimmed cape, on account of the cold.

"You *do* look smart, Mr Georgie," Diva told him by way of greeting. "Thank you so much for answering my little note and coming to see me."

"It sounds most mysterious and exciting," Georgie told her.

"Well, it depends on what you mean by 'exciting'. Come into the front room. Janet can bring us some tea, and I'll tell you all about it."

When Georgie had settled himself in the armchair, Diva handed him the latter that had

ELEVEN

arrived that morning. He put on his spectacles and began to read.

"It certainly does seem that he has developed a sudden interest in you," he remarked when he had come to the end, and re-read the letter.

"And I have no interest in him," Diva wailed. "What am I to do?"

Georgie considered the matter. "Surely that depends on what he says?"

"Well, supposing..." Diva hesitated, seemingly lost for words. "Supposing he asks me to marry him?"

"I suppose that is one possibility," Georgie admitted. "Well, you'd just have to tell him No, wouldn't you?"

"But I can't do that," Diva exclaimed. "I mean, it would just be too embarrassing for words, wouldn't it? Just imagine what you would feel if some stranger, even if they were famous, asked you to marry them – I mean if you weren't married to Lucia already. How would you feel then?"

Georgie, who had memories of a time in Riseholme when he was convinced that one, if not both, of the Misses Antrobus had had matrimonial designs on him, shuddered. "Yes, I do see what you mean. I suppose what we must do is to make sure that he never gets a chance to ask the question. I'll tell you what. Have you written a reply to his letter? No? Then we must make sure that he doesn't come to see you today. Tell him that you have a terrible cold and that you don't want to give it to him."

"Oh yes, that does sound like a good idea," said Diva.

"The nice thing about a cold is that it can last as long or as short a time as you want it to."

"I suppose so," said Diva. "If I write a little note telling him that I have a cold, you'll take it to him at Mallards, will you?"

"Of course."

"But then what happens if he wants to visit me even if I have a cold? Or waits here until I decide to get better?"

"May I tell Olga Bracely about this?" asked Georgie.

"I was hoping that you might say that, but I hardly dared to ask you."

"Good. Because what I will tell her is that he must not stay here too long. She and he must go in a few days at the very most."

"Oh, thank you. But will she listen to what you have to say?"

"I am sure she will if I explain the situation to her, and make her promise to keep it a secret."

"That's very kind of you."

ELEVEN

"But you must make sure that you don't go out of the house during that time. Janet must do all your marketing for you."

"Well, at least it's winter, so there won't be any tourists wanting teas. I was thinking of closing the tea-shop during the whole of January anyway."

"Very wise," said Georgie. "Now, as well as persuading Olga and Sasha – that is, Mr Abramov – to leave Tilling in the next few days or so, I will also speak to Sasha and tell him that his attentions are unwelcome to you."

"Oh, you are kind. If you do that, it will be a great weight off my mind. But please, not a word to Lucia about all this, if you please."

"That might be a little difficult. You know how she can get secrets out of you. Perhaps I shouldn't have said that, but it's true. But I will try, and if she does find out, I will make sure she understands that it must go no further. I shall be very firm about it."

TWELVE

Georgie returned to Mallards, conscious of the fact that he bore a great responsibility. Lucia would be better at this sort of thing than he, he felt, but he been enjoined not to discuss it with her, and he had every intention of keeping his word on the matter.

As soon as the opportunity arose, just before lunch, he drew Olga aside. "I have something very important I want to say to you," he said. "Something rather personal and private."

"It sounds exciting," Olga replied. "Do you think I shall like it?"

"I really don't know," Georgie said. "It's not about you, or me, or Lucia for that matter."

Twelve

"Let me guess," Olga said. "It's about Sasha and Diva, isn't it?"

"Yes, it is. How clever of you to guess."

"Not really. Sasha's been on at me all yesterday evening when we got back, even though it was after midnight, and again this morning trying to find out what he can about poor Mrs Plaistow. He wanted to write her a letter to tell her that he wanted to speak with her on a private matter."

"He wrote it and delivered it," Georgie told her.

"Oh dear," said Olga. "I'm very fond of Sasha – as a composer, that is – but he would make a terrible husband. As for me, I could never bear the sound of his attempts at singing, which he makes whenever he's had a drop too much, which, though I don't want it to go any further, happens a little too often for comfort. And any woman who married him would have to put up with endless tales of his youth in Russia."

"Rather like the Major in India."

"Exactly. Except that instead of tropical jungles, it would be birch forests, and instead of tigers, it would be bears. Believe me, I've only been working with him for a few months on the development of my part in his opera, and if I never see or hear of another birch tree for the rest of my life, or even catch a faint whiff of a bear ever again, I shall be happy."

"I see," said Georgie. He paused.

Olga smiled at him. "You know, it's rather amusing."

"What do you mean?"

"Do you remember, all that time ago in Riseholme – years and years it seems to be now – you and I made a little plot to bring Colonel Boucher and Mrs Weston together and to arrange a happy marriage for them? Well now, you and I are going have to work together to keep two people apart."

"I see what you mean. Yes, I suppose it is rather amusing, but not for poor Diva, or even Sasha, if it comes to that. I've told her she must catch a cold, but what else are we to do?"

"The first thing to do is to make sure that Sasha doesn't see Diva this afternoon. You and Lucia must take him with you out of Tilling for the afternoon, or for the whole evening if necessary. Get Cadman, isn't it? to take you all to see the sunset over the marshes or the church in Hastings or something. Just make sure that he has no chance to see Diva."

"Will you be coming with us?"

Olga shuddered. "Certainly not. As I said, I have had enough of bears and birch trees to last me for the rest of my life, and that's what you'll have all afternoon if I know Sasha."

"And what will you be doing?"

"I shall use Lucia's telephone to speak to the manager of Covent Garden. And he will then send a telegram to Sasha here stating that it is vital that he and I come to London as soon as possible – and imploring him to come tonight if it is possible, tomorrow if not. Believe me, Sasha really wants *Tsarina Ekaterina* to be performed there, and he'll do anything to make sure it happens."

"Can you really do that?"

"Oh yes, I am sure that Sir Philip will see things my way – that is, if he wants me to continue to perform there." She looked at Georgie's somewhat horrified expression. "Opera is a tough business, you know. It's not all dressing up and singing, and flowers from admirers at the stage door. You have to be ruthless at times if you want to succeed."

"Well, thank you very much for your help. I suppose I had better go and see Lucia and arrange for Sasha to be out of the house this afternoon."

THIRTEEN

In Grebe, Elizabeth was still somewhat at a loss as to how Lucia should be appropriately repaid for her perfidy in bringing a drunken Russian to her New Year party.

Benjy was, as she had expected, uncommunicative at breakfast, and drank quantities of tea, but refused his boiled egg. Her attempts to wish him a Happy New Year might as well have fallen on deaf ears, being acknowledged only by a faint grunting sound.

She had determined to start work on making the house ready for the New Year. This had the added advantage of being a rather noisy and disruptive process, thereby punishing her

Thirteen

Benjy-boy in a more subtle way than mere verbal chastisement would accomplish.

It had been tempting to take out her feelings on Benjy at breakfast, but on reflection, she considered that it was not wholly his fault that he had over-imbibed the previous evening. Nor, when she considered further, did it seem sensible to waste a perfectly good store of resentment on her husband when it could be so much more pleasurably directed against Lucia.

There remained a few boxes and tea-chests of chattels which had yet to be unpacked following the move from Mallards to Grebe. Indeed, there seemed to be some of Major Benjy's effects from when he moved into Mallards on the occasion of his marriage to Elizabeth.

She eagerly seized on this last in the hope that there would prove to be some interesting material that might prove useful at some future date. In one of the tea-chests there was a small box with characters on it that she believed to be Chinese. She opened the box to discover a mass of small white tiles, which might well have been ivory, marked with a mass of strange symbols, some bearing the same symbol as others.

"A game of some kind," she said to herself, and as she did so, a memory of something read a few months previously came to the surface. There was some sort of game that had come from China, and had taken the fashionable world by storm a few years previously, though it had not as yet reached Tilling. What was its name? 'Ma John' or something like that.

The faint flickerings of an idea were kindled in her mind. Abandoning the remaining contents of the tea-chest, Elizabeth took the box of tiles to the study, where Major Benjy was sprawled in his favourite armchair, eyes closed, snoring gently.

"Wake up, sleepy-head," she said to him playfully.

"Eh? What? Who?" he answered, rubbing his eyes, and heaving himself into a more upright position. "Must have dropped off, what?"

"What is this? I found it in one of the tea-chests in the box-room," his wife asked him, displaying the box that she had brought down with her.

He took it from her hands, and opened it, a look of puzzlement on his face. "Let me see now," he said slowly. "I haven't set eyes on this in years. I won this off old Blinky Haynes in the Mess in Lucknow. I bet him my silver cigar-case against this that he couldn't jump over four chairs and land on his feet." He chuckled.

Thirteen

"Silly fool went and twisted his ankle. Still, I got this from him."

"Yes, but what *is* it?"

"It's a Chinese game. Sort of like rummy, if I remember right. Old Blinky brought it with him from his stint in Hong Kong. Used to play it sometimes in the Mess. You need four people to play it." He picked up one of the tiles and appeared to study it. "This is a green dragon, I remember."

Elizabeth looked at it. It looked like a tangled mess of green lines to her.

"And this is a two of bamboos. These are suits, like cards. These are bamboos, these are coins and these are characters."

Elizabeth looked. "Interesting," she said. An idea was beginning to form in her mind. "Can you remember how you play it?"

"I can remember some of it," he said. "Scoring was dashed complicated. Blinky used to have to keep the scores. That's probably why he usually won, I suppose."

"What's it called? The game, I mean."

"Some sort of Chinese name. Mah-jong, I think that's what Blinky called it. It's all starting to come back now I see it again. Like I say, it was a dashed pleasant way to spend an evening. A few chota pegs and a few hands of mah-jong, and we'd have a rare old time of it. Why don't we try playing it here in Tilling some time? Might make a nice change from bridge, eh, Liz?"

The idea that had been forming in Elizabeth's mind suddenly burst forth full-fledged and fully armed, like Pallas Athena emerging from Zeus' brow.

Mah-jong was to be the new pastime for Tilling society, replacing bridge, which had long since lost its novelty for her (and she had good reason to believe, for others). She was to be the undisputed champion of this new game, with its mysterious Oriental associations. And best of all, Lucia would have no part in it. She would make sure of that.

FOURTEEN

Georgie approached Lucia and explained that it would be necessary for them to take Sasha out of Tilling for the afternoon.

"I can't tell you why," he said. "I promised that I wouldn't."

"I can guess," Lucia smiled. "And I won't even ask you to tell me if I'm right or wrong. Will Olga be coming with us?"

"She wants to stay here. She has a few things to arrange over the telephone."

"Very well. I think that today would be a good day to visit Battle, do you not? I shall inform Cadman to have the car ready immediately after luncheon. What time should we return, do you think?"

FOURTEEN

"After dark, certainly. That's quite early at this time of year."

After lunch, Georgie and Lucia, with Sasha firmly wedged between them, were seated in the back seat of Lucia's motor, well wrapped in blankets and rugs against the chill of the winter air. Foljambe had very thoughtfully provided hot-water-bottles for all of them, and had made sure that Cadman wore the warm woollen scarf that she had presented to him at Christmas.

Before setting out, Georgie had implored Cadman to take a route which kept them as far away from Wasters as possible. He had no wish for Sasha to see Diva's house as they were on their way.

During the journey, Sasha recounted in his broken English, as Olga had foretold, tales of bears in birch woods. At one point he attempted to sing, but Lucia, worried about the effect that the sound might have on Cadman's driving, instantly engaged him in conversation and prevented any possible accident.

At Battle, Georgie and Lucia took Sasha firmly in hand and conducted him on a tour of Battle Abbey, attempting to explain the significance of the Norman Conquest.

Sasha seemed puzzled. "I do not understand,"

FOURTEEN

he said. "I live in France many years now. Is beautiful country. Good food, beautiful women. This William, why he come to England? Look." He spread an expansive arm over the landscape. "Cold. How you say? Moist." Indeed the air was cold and damp, with more than a hint of mist and fog. "Food? In England I eat the worst food of my life. Not your house," he hurriedly added to Lucia. "But last night at that Mrs Mapp-Flint's house? And the drink? In Russia we would not give to dog. Pah!" He seemed about to spit, but apparently thought better of it. "And English women? So ugly." He pulled a face. "Not you, or Miss Bracely, or that Plaistow woman last night, of course. I ask again. Why this William come to England?"

To this there was no polite answer that could be given, and Lucia and Georgie determined to ignore it.

"It's not very polite of you to talk about English ladies like that," Georgie objected. "Though I must agree with you about last night's food and drink."

"Now, Georgie, we must be generous in spirit towards those who are not as fortunate as ourselves," Lucia told him, though there was a smile on her face.

"Is not like Russia," Sasha pronounced at

FOURTEEN

length. "Is very different." He seemed about to start singing again, but Lucia forestalled him.

"It will be dark soon," Lucia said. "I do not want Cadman to have to drive too far in the dark, so we must set off soon."

"I was just about to say the same thing," said Georgie.

Sasha had little choice but to follow his host and hostess, however unwillingly, and maintained a sullen silence throughout the journey back to Mallards.

Olga met them at the door, excitedly waving a telegram. "Sasha, I'm so glad you're back now. We must set off for London immediately. Look!" She thrust the telegram at him.

"I do not have glasses with me," Sasha grumbled. "You read."

"Addressed to you, Mr A.D.Abramov. 'Urgent that you come to London instantly to discuss problem with possible production of Tsarina Ekaterina. Philip Slocombe.'"

"But I do not understand!" Sasha said. "What is this word 'possible'? Sir Philip gave me promise that Ekaterina would be produced in spring. I must speak to him soon. He must give me my opera. He give his word!"

"Dear Lucia," said Olga. "I hope you don't mind, but I asked your maid Grosvenor, and I

Hugh Ashton – 75

Fourteen

asked Foljambe, Georgie, to pack up my things and Sasha's, and I took the liberty of checking the trains to London. There is an excellent one that leaves in forty-five minutes." She spoke rapidly in German to Sasha, who replied with an emphatic nod and "*Da, da*," which even Georgie was sure was the Russian for "Yes".

"Sasha agrees. In order to save his opera, he will have to leave."

"Of course, Cadman will drive you and your luggage to the station," Lucia told her.

"Thank you so much. I am so sorry that this visit has been so short, but I will make sure that when *Tsarina* appears on stage, you will have a pair of the best seats in the house."

"We look forward to it. Thank you, dear Olga," said Lucia. "I will just go and tell Cadman to take your luggage and cases to the car."

She left, and Olga drew Georgie to one side. "I'm ever so clever," she whispered to Georgie, "and ever so wicked, aren't I?"

"You're a marvel," he assured her. "I simply have no idea how you manage it."

"Practice," she replied simply. "But you and Lucia really must come and see me in London when I'm singing. And then I can take you to a splendid little Italian restaurant I've discovered, and introduce Lucia to all kinds of famous people – she'll love that, won't she? And we can have a jolly time together."

"It sounds lovely," Georgie told her. "I'm looking forward to it ever so much already."

Cadman appeared to tell them that the car was ready, and Lucia and Georgie saw their guests to the car, and waved them out of sight as the car drove off to the station.

"Now what was all that about?" said Lucia. "The trip to Battle, and the telegram from London?"

"I cannot tell you," Georgie said. "I promised. Tarsome, I know, but a promise is a promise."

"No tell ickle Lucia?"

"No," he said firmly. "So please don't ask."

"Very well," Lucia said. "Ickle *Mozartino*? First time this year."

"Oh, you do make it sound exciting. Let us see. Oh yes, that symphony arranged for four hands."

They seated themselves at the piano. "Looks dwefull diffy," said Lucia. "Me to take tweble? Ready? *Uno, duo, tre.*"

FIFTEEN

The next day at Grebe saw Elizabeth Mapp-Flint with her idea of mah-jong as Tilling's new pastime taking shape. The first difficulty was that she had no idea of the rules, and her husband had forgotten them, assuming that he had ever known them in the first place.

"There's a book somewhere," he said at breakfast when she mentioned this difficulty to him. "I won it from old Blinky when I won the set from him. Dashed if I can remember where I put it, though."

"Then after breakfast, I want you to go up to the box-room and find it," she said to him firmly.

"Very well. Probably find a lot of other hidden

treasures," he said. "Brought back a lot of good stuff from India. That tiger-skin which you used to trim your skirt with that time."

"I remember," Elizabeth said coldly. The occasion on which she had worn that garment was seared in her memory, and was unlikely ever to be forgotten by her. "And your riding-whip." That made them even, though a mystery still attached to the mysterious disappearance and subsequent reappearance of the whip, in contrast to the hairs on the strips of tiger-skin used to trim the green skirt which were not firmly attached at all and had long ago parted company with the garment.

Benjy made his way upstairs after breakfast. After an hour, in which time she heard bangs and thumps, Elizabeth considered going in to help him at his task, but eventually decided against it. Some things were better left unseen, she felt (though she fully intended to look after he had finished and see if there was anything that might be of interest or future value to her).

A little later, Benjy emerged, dusty, and with streaks of dirt across his face, brandishing a small volume.

"Found it, Liz," he proclaimed. "Right at the bottom of the last box."

She took it from him, and read the title. "A

FIFTEEN

Manual for those wishing to enjoy the Ancient Chinese Pastime of Mah-Jongg."

On a first perusal of the pages, she could see that the game offered many possibilities for creative interpretation of the rules – provided, that is, that the rules were interpreted by her.

"Thank you, Benjy-boy," she said, and took the book and box of tiles to the drawing-room, where she set up a card-table in order to examine the tiles more closely.

As Benjy had said, there were several sets of coins and sticks and Chinese characters. Then there were winds and dragons, all written in Chinese. She set herself to learn these quickly – the anticipated joy of being able to tell Diva the difference between a North and a South wind, or to explain to dear Susan that a Flower was not a Season, spurred her on.

In the middle of this, her husband came in. She thought she could detect a faint scent of whisky on his breath, but she decided to let sleeping dogs lie for the moment. They could always be woken later.

"Just learning the tiles, dear," she explained.

"I can remember a lot of it now," he said. "You start the game by building a wall, like this." He demonstrated, as she turned the pages of the book.

"Oh I see," she said. "How exciting." Together, they set up the tiles, referring to the book for guidance. "Definitely more interesting than shuffling and dealing cards for bridge, isn't it?"

She read on. "This does look wonderfully exciting and complicated," she said. "Oh, what fun we shall have, Benjy-boy!"

She settled in her chair, picking up tiles from the newly built wall, and arranging them in various groups as she turned the pages of the book.

"So I see," she said. "Yes, you can have sets and runs of tiles, and all these deliciously complicated scoring rules. Did you play for money when you played in India?"

"I should say we did! And old Blinky was always the one who came out on top. He was the one with the rule-book, eh?" He winked in an unpleasant and suggestive manner.

"I can see that we're going to have quite a lot of excitement with this," Elizabeth said. "I know that we are meant to have four people playing, but maybe you and I could practice a little? Just the two of us?"

"Why not, old girl? It will make a nice change from bridge, won't it?"

"Exactly," Elizabeth replied, with a hyaena smile.

Hugh Ashton – 81

SIXTEEN

It only took a few days before Elizabeth and her husband felt confident enough to hold their first mah-jong party.

For this initial session, invitations were sent to the Wyses, on the basis that if they were to accept the new pastime as an alternative to bridge, the rest of Tilling society would almost automatically fall in line behind them.

At two o'clock on the appointed day, therefore, Susan's Royce drew up outside Grebe, disgorging a sable-swathed Susan and her husband, who was clad in an elegant quilted maroon smoking-jacket and a soft-collared shirt, with a lilac silky cravat.

"Dear lady," he said to Elizabeth, with a

small bow. "How very honoured we are that you have invited us to be the first to engage in this fascinating new diversion that you have discovered."

"The honour is all ours," Elizabeth smiled, "in your acceptance of our invitation."

She led the small party into the drawing-room, where a card table was already set up, with the mysterious Chinese box on it. The book of rules was out of sight, but was conveniently to hand, from where it could be retrieved and consulted in the event of a dispute over rules – an unlikely event, to be sure, where the urbane Mr Wyse was a participant.

"But how did you come by this?" Susan asked when the box had been opened and the exotic tiles revealed.

"From my days in India. A brother-officer was my introduction to the game, and when I returned to this country, I naturally brought this with me," Benjy told him.

"You must be very patient with us," Mr Wyse told him. "We are, after all, rank beginners here, and you are by way of being something of an expert."

"Oh no, dear Mr Wyse," Elizabeth laughed gaily. "We are by no means experts." Though these words were nothing less than the truth,

SIXTEEN

the way in which they were expressed implied that they were not to be taken seriously.

Elizabeth explained the basic rules of the game, and how to build the wall, and battle commenced, punctuated by helpful and sometimes contradictory explanations at frequent intervals from Elizabeth.

At the end of the first hand, of which Elizabeth declared herself the winner, Susan Wyse spoke, for almost the first time that afternoon.

"Dear me, what an interesting and lovely game, if I may say so, Elizabeth. I was quite sure that I was going to find another green dragon, but he was in your hand all the time."

"Oh those naughty dragons!" said Elizabeth, smiling. "Mr Wyse, what are your thoughts regarding this game?"

"Most enjoyable indeed," he said. "Dear me," he added, looking at the score sheet by Elizabeth's elbow. "I am happy we were not playing for money. I would have seen a small fortune flowing into your purse, dear Mrs Mapp-Flint."

"Some tea, and then another hand?" suggested Elizabeth. Upon general agreement with this suggestion, she rang the bell for Withers, and soon the assembled company enjoyed tea, sardine sandwiches, and a plate of coco-nut jumbles.

"Now, another game?" said the Major. To sounds of general agreement, the wall was once again constructed, and play commenced. This time, Elizabeth allowed herself to make several mistakes, and chose not to capitalise on errors committed by her opponents, with the result that, to her great surprise, Susan Wyse found herself the winner.

"Beginner's luck," she modestly fluttered.

"No, no, I will have none of that," Elizabeth protested. "Masterly play, wouldn't you say, Benjy?"

"Oh yes, indeed," he answered, though he was as confused as Susan herself as to how the result had been achieved.

"Do we have time for another game, Algernon?" asked Susan. "That is," she added hurriedly, "if Elizabeth has no objection."

"I see no reason why we should not, always provided, that is, that our hostess and hostess are kind enough to permit us to stay."

"With the greatest of pleasure, what?" said the Major. "Mr Wyse, a small whisky and soda to take away the cold of the East Wind, ha ha?"

"Most kind of you to offer, but I feel I must decline."

Sixteen

Having offered liquid refreshment to his guest, Benjy felt justified in pouring a drink for himself. To be sure, it was rather larger than the one he would have offered his guest, had Mr Wyse accepted, but given that Mr Wyse had declined the offer, he felt entitled to his guest's share as well as his own. Meanwhile Elizabeth had rung for more tea, and play resumed.

This time Elizabeth won easily. To be sure, the tiles she needed fell into her hand as required, but a smart slap on the wrist to Benjyboy, caused by his attempt to make a run of four tiles, which she was sure was contrary to the rules (and she was subsequently proved to be correct by reference to the rule book) and speedy snapping up of unconsidered trifles in the form of the unforced errors made by her inexperienced opponents ensured her a very considerable and convincing win.

"We must look to our laurels, Susan," said Mr Wyse, as the sables were fetched and draped around Mrs Wyse. "A most enjoyable and instructive game, Mrs Mapp-Flint. I do trust that it will prove to be the first of many such."

"Oh, so do I, Mr Wyse, so do I," smiled Elizabeth as she ushered her guests to the door.

SEVENTEEN

Mah-jong was clearly a 'starter', to use Benjy-boy's term, and Elizabeth allowed a day for Susan to spread the word about this new pastime (she did not expect Mr Wyse to partake of anything as vulgar as gossip, though he could sometimes be relied on to impart an air of veracity to rumours that it was to Elizabeth's advantage to be believed).

Her foresight was rewarded when the Padre greeted her outside Twistevant's where she was bound to order some leeks ("so tasty and nutritious" and a large turnip "economical and filling").

"What ho, Mistress Mapp!" he proclaimed. "I

Seventeen

hear tell from Mistress Wyse that ye have discovered a bonny new game from the Orient."

"Oh, dear," said Elizabeth. "That was meant to be a secret. My Benjy and I are beginners at the game, and we wanted no-one to know until we felt ourselves worthy to show our faces in public, so to speak."

"Hoots! She told me that your mannie and you were fair maisters and mistresses of this thing. Now what is it y-clept? She said the name to me, and it's fair gone out of my poor noggin."

"Mah-jong," Elizabeth said firmly. "But as for Benjy and I being masters and mistresses of the game, did dear Susan not tell you that she won a hand against us?"

"Aye, that she did," the Padre admitted.

Elizabeth waited for the expected request.

"Wee wifie and I were thinking," he began hesitantly. "Perhaps we might be permitted a wee peek at this new mah-jong? Just a wee peek, ye ken."

"Let me think," answered Elizabeth, making a brave show of actually doing so. "Today? No, impossible, I'm afraid. But tomorrow, if you and Evie can come to Grebe, say at half-past two, Benjy and I will be happy to introduce the elements of the game to you. No more than the bare elements, I am afraid."

"Two and a half of the clock on the morrow? Aye, I do believe that wee wifie and I will be able to pay ye a visit then."

"Until tomorrow, then," smiled Elizabeth, and went in to purchase her vegetables.

As she came out, having had an entirely satisfactory altercation with Twistevant on the state of the carrots with which he had supplied her just after Christmas, she spied Diva, moving at great speed in her general direction.

"Good morning, Diva dear," she said, as the regular motion of her legs, so like a mechanical doll's, came to a stop. "Going somewhere in a hurry?"

"Just wanted to ask." Diva panted. "Susan. The other day at Grebe."

"Susan Wyse? Oh yes, she and Algernon were kind enough to pay us a visit the other day."

"Some new game. Chinese or something."

Elizabeth furrowed her brow in pretended thought. "Ah yes. Benjy-boy discovered one of his treasures that he had brought back from India, oh so long ago, it must have been, and he and I have been amusing ourselves with it a little."

"A most interesting game, Susan says. Makes a change from bridge."

"Do you know, I think she may be correct for

SEVENTEEN

once. Bridge has become a little *de trop*, don't you think? That means 'too much' in French."

"Thank you for the lesson," Diva retorted. "If you mean there has been too much arguing over revokes and false deals and scoring, I must agree with you." This was intended as an attack on Elizabeth's method of playing bridge, which could be described as being more than argumentative. Indeed, it was positively aggressive in its claims of perceived slights and losses, and the attack was duly recognised as such.

"Diva, dear, old friends as we are, I would hardly dare to criticise the way that you zealously scoop up your pennies after each rubber—" Elizabeth began, but she was interrupted halfway.

"—but you are about to do exactly that," a red-faced Diva retorted.

Elizabeth opened her mouth to deliver a stinging rebuke, but immediately thought better of it. This was not the time for her to be making enemies. "Nothing further from my mind, dear," she simpered. "I was going to ask you if you would like to join Benjy-boy and me for a few hands of this new game? Say, Friday, at half-past two?"

This, of course, was the fish for which Diva

had been angling, and she hauled it out of the water and landed it with pleasure.

"Delighted, Elizabeth. But who will make up the fourth? Susan says that you need four people for the game."

"I think quaint Irene might be interested, don't you? I shall pop into Taormina on my way home and leave an invitation."

"You'll be wasting your time," Diva told her. "She's not there."

"What can you mean?"

"She's in London. Opera. Designing costumes and scenery. Went off yesterday. With Olga Bracely and that drunken Russian. Hah! Sooner her than me."

There was some salt here for the taking, ready to be rubbed into the wound, but with a heroic effort, Elizabeth turned her back on the temptation. "How vexing," she said. "I shall find a fourth, never fear, and we'll have a jolly afternoon of it together."

Diva trotted off, seemingly content with having achieved her objective, leaving Elizabeth unsure as to how to arrange Diva's game. It was impossible to invite one of the Wyses on their own, likewise the Padre or Evie alone. The curate, although she had taken a dislike to him on account of the way that he pronounced

SEVENTEEN

his 'R's – in a fashion that she had pronounced "foreign" – was, however, a possibility.

It was a ten-minute detour to reach the street near the station where the curate lived and moved and had his being, and her crossness at this unnecessary trek and the consequent return journey was increased by her being informed that the curate would be busy with a meeting of the Mothers' Union on the proposed date.

There was, she gloomily concluded as she trudged back to town, always the possibility of inviting Georgie Pillson to take part, while pointedly excluding Lucia. That course of action might actually prove to be more satisfying. However, on the principle of "first catch your hare", she would have to catch him at some time when he was not with Lucia.

It was too cold to wait around near the door of Mallards on the off-chance that he might appear, so luck would have to play a larger part in this matter than she would otherwise have preferred.

And that day, Lady Luck was smiling. Arrayed in a smart new overcoat with a fur collar turned up against the chill wind, Georgie Pillson came walking towards her, having turned around the corner that led to the haberdasher's.

SEVENTEEN

"Mr Georgie!" Elizabeth greeted him. "Are you well?"

"Thank you, yes," he replied. "But it's most tarsome. They promised me that in the New Year they would have that turquoise silk that I need for my new cushion cover, and now they tell me it won't be here until February. It's too bad. All they have is a blue-green silk which is hidjus. Won't do at all."

"Well, maybe I have some good news for you," Elizabeth smiled. "Major Benjy has discovered a new game that he brought from India–"

"Oh yes, Susan Wyse was telling me all about it yesterday. It sounds most exciting. Winds and dragons and things."

"–and I am giving a little party to play the game on Friday at half-past two," she went on, exactly as if Georgie hadn't interrupted her. Just Diva and you and Major Benjy and me. Four is the perfect number for mah-jong. Do say you'll be there."

"Well, I'm pretty certain that I won't be doing anything else at that time, so I am very happy to accept."

"So cosy. So happy. Then I will see you on Friday. *Au reservoir.*"

EIGHTEEN

"Really, Georgie," Lucia said when he told her of Elizabeth Mapp-Flint's invitation. "Are you sure that she didn't include me in the invitation?"

"Quite sure. She said four was the perfect number for mah-jong."

"I see. Yes, I seem to remember at Adele Brixton's the time that I stayed there, there were four at the table." Lucia sniffed. "Well, you can tell me all about it when you come back. Susan Wyse was quite taken with it when she talked to me, but I couldn't make head or tail of her explanation, and if you ask me, neither could she."

"I'm sure she didn't really want to invite me,"

said Georgie. "You can tell with Elizabeth when she's doing something that she really doesn't want to do. Her face goes all screwed up on one side, and she talks a bit faster than usual. I'm sure she wanted to invite Irene, but since Irene's gone off to London to work on Sasha's opera, she couldn't."

"It must be said," Lucia admitted, "that it was remarkably kind of Olga to invite Irene. There must be many other artists who would welcome the chance to work on a great masterpiece such as this opera of Mr Abramov's promises to be."

"Yes, but the other artists haven't painted the Picture of the Year at the Royal Academy, have they? Irene is as much a feather in their cap as they are in hers."

"I confess that I had not considered the matter in that light. An excellent point, Georgie. Well, no matter. I hope that you will enjoy yourself at Grebe."

"And what will you do?"

"I shall be improving my mind with that new history of the Doges of Venice. Or possibly practise the new Schubert that arrived just before Christmas. Dear me, how time flies. Where has it gone?"

NINETEEN

Georgie returned from his mah-jong session on the Friday evening with a look of some concern on his face.

"Did oo not like Liblib's little game, then?" asked Lucia. There was a certain tone of satisfaction in her voice.

"On the contrary," said Georgie. "It is a most enjoyable game in itself. It is Elizabeth herself that you must consider."

"I, Georgie? I must consider Elizabeth? Why?"

"Do you not see? She is planning to take over and run Tilling society, just as she did before we – I mean you – arrived here."

"Georgie, are you implying that I somehow

lead Tilling society? Why, Algernon Wyse with his connections to Italian nobility, and Susan Wyse with her Order surely must be regarded as the leaders of Tilling society. Not to mention Elizabeth herself, who lived in this very house for so long and is so much a part of Tilling."

"You are being ridiculous," Georgie told her firmly. "Who was made Councillor, and then appointed as Mayor? It wasn't Mr Wyse or Susan, or Elizabeth. Whose garden-parties does everyone attend? And whose dinner-party invitations are eagerly awaited by all who matter in this town? It is perfectly absurd for you to pretend otherwise."

"There may be some truth in what you say."

"Of course there is, or I wouldn't be saying it. This mah-jong of Elizabeth's is a 'stunt', and it is her aim to make it replace bridge, and Grebe to replace Mallards as the place for us all to meet."

"You may have a point there."

"Indeed I do. I tell you that if she continues in this way, every time we invite a party to Mallards for bridge, we will find that they have already accepted an invitation to play mah-jong at Grebe."

"Then what are we to do? Am I to somehow

NINETEEN

learn this ridiculous game and set myself up against her? Is that what you are saying?"

"No, you must rise above her. She cheats, anyway."

"I am shocked to hear you make such an accusation, Georgie," Lucia reprimanded him. There was a pause. "How do you mean?"

"Because she and Major Benjy are the only ones who seem to know the rules, everyone must do what she says. Only I am sure that sometimes she says one thing and then says something completely opposite a little later."

"Were you playing for money? I have heard, I am sure, that this game is often an excuse for gambling."

"We weren't, but I don't think that is the point. Elizabeth simply wants to win and be on top."

"Then the answer is clear," Lucia said after a little thought. "We must learn this game, and learn it properly, and then perhaps we should teach Elizabeth."

"That doesn't sound like a very good idea to me. It would simply look as though we were copying her. No, what we must do is to find something original that will continue to keep you as the queen of Tilling."

"And you as king?" laughed Lucia.

"Well, I suppose so, yes. Or rather, a Prince Consort."

"Do you have any suggestions?"

"As a matter of fact, I do. When I was coming back from Grebe, I suddenly knew what the answer was. It's croquet."

Lucia laughed. "Are you prepared to wait until summer, then? The weather forecast is for snow tomorrow, and it is far too cold to stay outdoors for any length of time."

"Of course you are right," Georgie said. "But this is where I think I have been rather clever, though I say it myself. You can buy miniature croquet sets that allow you to play on a table, like that rather nice mahogany table which is in the garden-room and only has a few photographs on it at the moment. So we could arrange little croquet-parties in the winter, and we could set out a croquet court in the garden in summer."

"I have to say, Georgie my dear, that it does sound fun, and I think that more people will be happier coming to Mallards for what sounds like a very enjoyable afternoon's entertainment than making their way out into the marshes to play some strange Chinese game." She paused. "Where does one find this miniature croquet, though?"

NINETEEN

"When I was last in London, I saw a set in a shop in Regent Street, but for the life of me I can't remember the name of the shop now. But if I send a telegram to Olga in London, she should be able to find a set and have it dispatched to us."

"And you thought of all this on the way back from Grebe? Well, that is clever of you."

"Actually, I did more than think of it. I sent the telegram from the Post Office on my way home. Maybe our croquet will appear tomorrow or perhaps on Monday."

TWENTY

As it turned out, it was Monday before the box appeared from London, addressed to Georgie, who eagerly unwrapped and opened it, examining the contents.

"Look at these," he said, waving a tiny mallet in his hand. "And these," pointing to the hoops that he was already arranging on the table.

"Be careful," Lucia warned him. "We don't want to scratch the table."

"I'll be very careful," Georgie assured her.

He placed one of the marble-sized balls on the table and made a very gentle experimental stroke with the mallet. The ball moved a little faster than he had expected, and rolled off the edge of the table onto the floor.

TWENTY

"Tarsome," he said, bending down and retrieving it from where it had rolled. After a few more strokes, he decided that it might be better to play on a tablecloth rather than the polished wood, and remarked as much to Lucia, who had been watching with interest.

"Very well," she said, "and it will also protect the surface of the table," and rang for Grosvenor, to whom she gave instructions to bring a cloth for the table. "But not starched," she instructed.

"Very good, madam," Grosvenor said, and left to return a few minutes later with a piece of green baize which she, with Georgie's help, spread over the table.

"Much better," he said, after a few experimental shots. "Look," as he made a particularly difficult croquet shot which sent one ball through a hoop and dispatched the other skittering to the opposite end of the table.

"Oh, this does look like fun," said Lucia, by now unable to resist, taking another of the miniature mallets, and tapping away at the other end of the table.

After a few minutes, Lucia proposed a game between her and Georgie, a challenge which he readily accepted.

It soon became clear that while Georgie was

by far the more accurate player of the two, Lucia's skill lay in the tactics of the game – a skill which was let down by her mis-shots and lack of control. Several times Georgie was forced to hunt under the table for one of Lucia's balls which had rushed past its goal off the edge of the table and rolled to what invariably seemed to be the most inaccessible spot on the floor.

The game ended in a near-draw, with Lucia's second ball hitting the final post just before Georgie's turn, which would have made him the winner.

"Highly satisfactory," said Lucia. "Almost as much fun as the outdoor game."

"More fun," said Georgie. "No bending down in the hot sun. No worms. And you're not always looking for weeds in the flower-beds out of the corner of your eye when it's not your turn."

"Another game?" said Lucia. She looked at her watch. "It will have to be after luncheon. Do you realise, Georgie, that last game took us nearly an hour? What a pleasant morning it has been, but oh, dear me. No *musica*, no reading, and I am sure there are many letters to which I must reply. Me is vewy idle girl. Oo must scold naughty Lucia."

Twenty

"I shall do no such thing. As for me, there is certainly a letter that I must write," said Georgie. "To Olga to thank her so much for arranging this purchase for us."

TWENTY-ONE

The next stage in Lucia's strategic plan, as proposed by Georgie, was to recruit new supporters to her plan of making croquet an alternative to mah-jong.

She followed Elizabeth's thinking (though if she had been aware that she was doing so, she would have instantly taken a different course of action) in believing the Wyses to be the most influential in the spreading of new ideas throughout Tilling society.

However, she differed from Elizabeth by arranging for the game to take place in the evening, following a somewhat sumptuous dinner, rather than a meagre spread of lukewarm

Twenty-one

tea, underfilled sandwiches, and dry jumbles and cakes.

The invitation to dinner that she sent to her guests had at the bottom the mysterious legend, '*una piccola sorpresa*' – thereby giving them warning that something unexpected would be part of the evening.

"Are you going to serve lobster *à la Riseholme*?" asked Georgie.

Lucia considered and smiled. "I think not – there are good reasons for reserving it for occasions when Elizabeth will be present. No, we shall have a nice wild duck from Rice's. He told me he was expecting some to come in tomorrow."

TWENTY-TWO

The Wyses arrived promptly, as always, and after Susan's sables had been removed, and her new dress duly admired by Georgie and Lucia, the company sat down to dinner.

The course of the conversation turned (with a little light touch on the tiller by Lucia) to China, and from China to mah-jong, and from there to Elizabeth Mapp-Flint.

"But is it possible," Susan asked, "that you have not gone to Grebe to play?"

"Georgie has played once, but so far I, alas, have been denied the pleasure of partaking in a game. I have only heard Georgie's version of events. May I ask you to tell me how you have found this mah-jong to be?"

TWENTY-TWO

This was something that Susan was only too pleased to do, and it carried the party through the soup and fish and into the duck. At length, even Susan Wyse found she had little more to say on the matter, and Lucia deftly steered the conversation to quaint Irene's being asked to design the scenery and the costumes for the new opera.

"A veritable triumph for Tilling," said Mr Wyse, raising his glass, presumably to Irene, or possibly to Tilling. "We are so fortunate to have such an accomplished and famous – justly so, I may add – addition to our society here."

"Though one cannot help but look somewhat askance at her dress and her manners at times," Susan added.

"We must make allowances for genius," Lucia smiled.

"I will grant you that Miss Bracely may be included in that number," Susan said. "But that funny little man with her. Russian, was he not? I do not understand what in the world he was doing with her, famous composer or not. And that scene with poor Mrs Plaistow. I can tell you, I hardly knew where to look."

"Most embarrassing," Mr Wyse agreed. "But all seems to be well now, I trust?" He bowed slightly towards Lucia and Georgie.

108 – A Tilling New Year

"Oh yes, very well indeed, thank you," Georgie assured him.

During the dessert (figs *à la Capri*, served in honour of Mr Wyse's sister, the Contessa de Faraglione), the subject of the *piccola sorpresa* was breached.

"Algernon and I are most intrigued," Susan told Lucia. "Perhaps there is something new that you have to show us?"

"Indeed so. After we have finished our coffee, I propose a game of croquet."

"Dear Mrs Pillson," exclaimed Mr Wyse. "It is now dark outside, and the weather— well, snow was forecast for tonight. You surely are not proposing that we go outside and play croquet?"

"By no means," said Lucia. "We can keep warm and dry, but still enjoy a game. But I say no more for now."

"You intrigue me," said Mr Wyse. "I eagerly anticipate the revelation of this mystery."

As promised, after the coffee had been drunk, Lucia led her way into the garden-room, where the table stood, prepared for the game that was about to commence. The older cloth that had been used at first had been replaced by a new green baize cloth, ordered by Lucia from the drapers, and cut to size.

"I see," said Mr Wyse, examining one of the

TWENTY-TWO

tiny mallets. "Most ingenious. Susan, my dear, this promises to be a most interesting evening."

"You have played before – on a lawn, I mean?" Georgie asked.

"Indeed I have. In fact, I represented my college when I was at University," Mr Wyse informed them. "I take it that the rules here are the same as they would be out there?" He gestured towards the garden.

"Indeed they are."

"Then let us start. Susan, my dear, we shall play together against our host and hostess."

It was a revelation for Georgie and Lucia to see the usually urbane and reserved Mr Wyse in such a state of excitement. He removed his velvet smoking jacket, and took a few experimental taps of the balls with his mallet before declaring that he was ready to start.

It soon became clear that he was a master of the tactics and strategy needed for the game, and poor Georgie soon found his ball being hit all over the table by Mr Wyse's finely-judged strokes.

Sooner than they had expected, and more than a little surprised, Lucia and Georgie found themselves the losers.

"Most enjoyable," said Mr Wyse. "I had no idea that such a thing," he indicated the table,

TWENTY-TWO

"was possible. Susan, we must consider a similar purchase for our home." He showed obvious signs of wanting to play again. This time, he and Georgie played against Lucia and Susan, and won even more easily than the previous game, almost entirely due to Mr Wyse's skill.

"And now," proposed Mr Wyse, flushed with his victory and addressing Lucia, "if you will permit me to partner you, dear lady..."

Lucia and Mr Wyse soon finished the game against Susan and Georgie.

"I must apologise," Mr Wyse said to Lucia as he put on his smoking jacket, and accepted a glass of port from Georgie. "The thrill of the competition makes me forget my manners."

"Not at all. It was an education to play against you."

"Very kind of you to say so." He pulled out his watch. "My word, is that the time? Well, Susan, we should be going. Many thanks for a most enjoyable evening."

Susan was poured into her sables, and the Wyses' Royce bumped its way a few hundred yards down the street.

"A success, do you think, *Georgino*?" Lucia asked Georgie.

"We made Mr Wyse happy, at least," he answered.

Hugh Ashton – 111

Twenty-two

"And he will tell the whole of Tilling what an enjoyable evening he has just spent," Lucia smiled.

TWENTY-THREE

Lucia was correct in her assumption. Mr Wyse, usually a rather reticent personality, was almost voluble in his accounts of the pleasurable evening he had spent at Mallards. He was very careful not to allude to his own prowess in the pastime he had enjoyed, but let it be understood that his host and hostess, not to mention his wife, had displayed great skill in their play.

The news of Lucia's innovation soon reached Elizabeth's ears. Though she was envious of the attention that was attracted, she still very much wanted to take part in this new experience herself, if only to be able to ridicule it later to her friends. She wondered if it was

Twenty-three

going to be necessary to invite Lucia to play mah-jong to secure the invitation to play table croquet, but concluded that the risk was not worth taking, since she was concerned that Lucia would simply laugh her efforts to scorn. She was therefore forced to content herself with the reports that came from Grebe from those lucky enough to be invited.

The next to take part were the Padre and Evie. For this occasion, Lucia did not serve as elaborate a dinner as had been provided for the Wyses, but the fare was of a more elaborate kind than her guests usually endured at their own home.

Of course, the surprise that had awaited the Wyses was no surprise to the Padre and Evie, but even so, they were most taken with the idea.

"'Tis a bonny wee thing," said the Padre, holding the miniature mallet. "I ween a body could drive a fair way with this one."

"Your golf should help you, Padre," said Lucia.

"Aye, it does seem to be akin to putting," he agreed.

Evie, for her part, was exclaiming over the whole concept. "Such a wonderful idea, Lucia dear. So pleasant to enjoy the game indoors, no matter what the weather."

"Well, shall we play?" suggested Georgie. "Padre, why don't you and Lucia play against Evie and me for the first game?"

The game soon came to a halt, as the Padre and Georgie found that they disagreed on the rule regarding taking extra strokes following a successful croquet. Eventually the matter was settled (to Georgie's satisfaction and the discomfiture of the Padre) by Lucia's consultation of the encyclopaedia entry on croquet. The result was that the Padre subsequently failed to concentrate sufficiently, and many of his shots went wild. Indeed, at one point he was forced to lie nearly flat on the floor to retrieve a ball which had cannoned off the table to lie underneath a bookcase.

Evie continued to play calmly and competently, with the result that she and Georgie managed a comfortable victory over their opponents.

"Again?" suggested Lucia. "Perhaps you gentlemen would like to ally yourselves against Evie and me?"

The challenge was accepted, but once again the Padre found himself on the losing side, while his wife could now claim two victories.

"I dinna ken what's come over me," he exclaimed, between sips of the restorative port

Twenty-three

that Georgie had poured for him. "When I was a wee bairn, I knew how to play this game. It's playing on this wee bitty table, I reckon."

The third match, however, between Evie and the Padre on the one hand, and Lucia and Georgie on the other, saw a marked improvement in his play, and the visitors chalked up a victory over their hosts.

"Aye, 'tis a bonny game," admitted the Padre, his good temper now seemingly restored. "I ween we should perhaps play for bawbees, in the same fashion as we do for bridge. Aye, and a few more games like that, and the poor of the parish would thank ye."

As the visitors were ushered out of the house, Lucia could make out the excited squeaks of Evie, wondering aloud where she and the Padre might procure a set of table croquet.

"Highly satisfactory, Georgie," she said as she closed the front door. "Evie winning tonight will definitely put the cat among the pigeons, as will the next game."

"Diva, of course. But who else will you invite?"

"Major Benjy, naturally. Don't you see, Elizabeth invited you without me, and I shall simply be returning the compliment."

"Well, that will also put the cat right in the middle of the pigeons, won't it?"

TWENTY-FOUR

At Grebe, Elizabeth was incensed by the thought that Benjy should be invited without her when the invitation arrived in the early morning post.

"Turn about is fair play, Liz," he pointed out at the breakfast table, in a vain attempt to calm the storm. "You invited Pillson without his wife, after all."

"That has nothing to do with it," Elizabeth angrily replied. "I call it downright impolite and ungrateful. I invited her to the New Year's Eve party, after all, and she repaid my hospitality by inviting that opera singer, who is no better than she should be, I am sure–"

"Fine-looking woman for all that," muttered

Twenty-Four

her husband, in a tone that would have been inaudible, except to his wife's finely-honed ears.

"Her looks are exactly what I am talking about," she retorted. "And that scruffy-looking Russian, if that's what he was, making eyes at Diva." She laughed scornfully. "Diva indeed! And then him dragging you off and his disgraceful drunken behaviour! And yours!" she added. "I am not sure that I shouldn't forbid you to visit Mallards. Who knows what might happen there?"

"Very well, I shan't go. I shall play golf with the Padre."

"You will do no such thing. You will go to Lucia's and you will report back to me what you see."

"I don't understand – I thought you didn't want me to go."

"Of course I want you to go. I want you to see what sort of nonsense she is up to. And don't drink too much while you're there."

"Hmph."

"I don't know what you mean by that noise."

Since the Major was unable to express the meaning of his snort in polite terms, he refrained from answering, but turned to his newspaper.

Twenty-four

"Ha!" he exclaimed. "Listen to this, Liz. 'We learn that Miss Irene Coles, the artist responsible for the Royal Academy's Picture of the Year a few years ago, a delicious satire of Boticelli's 'Birth of Venus', has been engaged by Covent Garden Opera House to advise on the design of the sets and the costumes for Mr Alexander Abramov's forthcoming opera, *Tsarina Ekaterina*, in which the celebrated prima-donna Miss Olga Bracely is expected to play the leading role.' And there's a photograph of Miss Bracely, and Abramov, and even one of Irene. See." He passed his newspaper over to Elizabeth who studied it with a corrugated brow.

"Very nice for them," she remarked, with more than a drop of acid in her tones. "It's a pity they couldn't get Irene to take that foul pipe out of her mouth when they took the picture of her. She is determined to be quaint, is she not, even for such a prestigious event as this. And that picture of Miss Bracely – she looks a perfect guy in that outfit. Oh, I see, she is meant to be Brünhilde. I'm glad I have never seen that opera, though of course it is the sort of thing that Lucia pretends to appreciate. And then the picture of that composer, oh dear. I doubt if there is a photographer in the

Twenty-four

country who could take a flattering portrait of him." She attacked the top of her boiled egg with more force than was strictly necessary for its dismemberment. "Still, I expect that dear Lucia will feel proud that her guests have their pictures in the paper."

TWENTY-FIVE

Lucia's reception for Diva and the Major was on the same scale as that for the Padre and Evie.

"Excellent eating," said the Major as he attacked his pork chop in a fashion that bore more than a faint resemblance to a starving tiger. "Don't often see a fine piece of meat like this at home, you know, though that mustn't go any further, what? A most tasty meal, Mrs Pillson. "

"I must agree with you there, Major," said Diva. "What delicious vegetables, Lucia. Are they from your garden? I don't remember seeing those carrots at Twistevant's."

"Indeed they are, Diva dear. I have all the

Twenty-Five

garden-produce I require now." There was a silence as the guests cast their minds back to Elizabeth's perfidy at the time she had rented Mallards to Lucia several summers previously, taking all the garden-produce for herself to sell to Twistevant's, while retaining that from Wasters, which she had rented from Diva, for her own use.

"Other than oranges and pine-apples and the like, of course," Georgie added. "We find it hard to grow those," he laughed. "More wine, Major?"

"Thank you, yes. *Quai hai!*"

The meal proceeded smoothly, and afterwards the guests were led into the garden-room, where they admired the croquet court laid out on the table.

"What fun!" exclaimed Diva. "I don't think I've played croquet since I was a girl. Never played indoors, though." She took one of the mallets and attempted to knock a ball it through the first hoop. "Oh dear, it's a lot more difficult than it looks, isn't it?" she said after half a dozen failed attempts.

"Never mind," Georgie told her encouragingly. "Once you've got the knack, it's very easy."

Meanwhile at the other end of the table, the Major was also in possession of a mallet.

However, he was having even less success than Diva. "Missed the bl— the blessed thing again," he said for the fifth time. "Seems to me that the table keeps moving." In fact it was the Major himself who was moving involuntarily, almost certainly a result of the wine he had drunk earlier in the evening. "Ha!" he said as he eventually managed to get a ball through the hoop. "Just a matter of keeping my eye on the ball, what?"

"Are we ready for a game?" Lucia asked. "Major Benjy and I against Diva and Georgie?"

"Delightful," said the Major. "Positive pleasure to play with you, Mrs Pillson. We'll show those blighters what's what, eh?" He seemed about to slap Lucia on the back in a comradely fashion, but some sense of prudence seemed to stay his arm at the last moment.

The game was not a smooth one, nor was it short. At least half the time seemed to be spent looking for the Major's ball, which appeared to have developed a talent for rolling into inaccessible places. For her part, Diva seemed to be suffering from a severe case of nerves, which meant that none of her shots went where she wanted.

"Oh dear oh dear oh dear," she wailed as she

missed a hoop from a distance of only a few inches. "So sorry, Mr Georgie."

"Never mind," said her partner.

At length the seemingly interminable game came to an end, and by that time, no one really seemed to care who it was who had won (the winners were declared to be Georgie and Diva, the Major's last shot having cannoned off the mantelpiece to come to rest under the piano).

Diva looked at her watch. "Dear me, is that the time? I really should be going home."

The Major showed no immediate signs of leaving, but Georgie steadfastly ignored his pointed glances towards the whisky decanter, and eventually the Major set course for Grebe. "A fine night," he remarked as he wrapped his scarf around him to protect him from the chill wind sweeping over the marshes.

"Indeed," said Georgie. "A very good night to you."

TWENTY-SIX

"I am surprised at Lucia wasting her time with such rubbish," Elizabeth said to her husband the next morning at breakfast after he had recounted the previous evening's events to her. "I would have thought that even she could have discovered something a little more productive. Perhaps learning the other movements of that mouldy old 'Moonlight Sonata'?"

"Wretched evening," said the Major. "Food was all right, though, and the wine, what there was of it, was very passable indeed." He sneezed twice. "I am sure I've caught a cold walking back from there last night."

"I do not know why she did not offer you the

TWENTY-SIX

use of her car and chauffeur to drive you back here."

"To be fair to her, Liz, it was a little late, and her chauffeur had probably gone to bed by that time."

"Well, she should have planned things better so that you didn't have to walk all that way in the dark. Or ordered a taxi to wait for you until you were ready to come home." She took a bite of toast. "Any more news about our Irene and Lucia's friends?"

"Haven't seen anything. Lot of fuss over nothing, if you ask me," said the Major. "Are we playing mah-jong today?"

"I am expecting the Padre and Evie at half-past two. I suggest that today we play for small stakes. I have worked out how the winnings should be calculated, in accordance with the scores."

"It will add a little spice to the game," Benjy remarked.

TWENTY-SEVEN

Indeed, the spice added to that afternoon's games was sufficient to flavour one of the Major's favourite curries. The Padre accepted the offer of Elizabeth's stakes with alacrity, but the first game soon saw him in debt to his hostess.

The next game also saw Elizabeth as the winner, and this time it was Evie who paid the price.

"Aye, and we must be getting a set for ourselves, and some instruction on how to play this bonny game for ourselves," the Padre remarked to his wife.

"There's nothing like practice and experience to build proficiency," said Elizabeth, mixing the tiles preparatory to building the wall for another game.

"I may be a wee bitty confused," said the Padre after a few rounds of the next game had been played, "but I mind you picked up a tile of a run – a 'chow' did you name it? – out of turn in the last game, but now you are saying that it is not permitted for me to do so?" His speech became less and less flavoured with Scottish and medieval terms as the sentence progressed.

It was indeed true that Elizabeth was guilty of contradicting herself, and furthermore, that she was well aware of what she had done. "Oh no, dear Padre," she babbled. "When one is playing as East Wind, as I was last game, it is perfectly permissible to pick up out of turn. Otherwise, I am afraid, no."

She would have to remember this new rule, she told herself. Or perhaps forget that she had ever said any such thing – which would be easier.

In any event, the Padre won that game, though it transpired that both Elizabeth and the Major had only required one tile each to complete a winning hand – in fact, they both required the same tile. The Padre's hand, however, was a high-scoring one, and it meant that he was now owed a not inconsiderable sum of money by his hostess.

Fortunes swayed back and forth between the visitors and their host and hostess, but at the end of the afternoon – indeed, the evening had set in almost without their noticing – Elizabeth was the overall winner.

"A most enjoyable afternoon, Mistress Mapp-Flint," the Padre said. "I look forward to our next game."

TWENTY-EIGHT

For the next few weeks, Tilling society found its time divided between Grebe and Mallards, partaking of the new and delightful diversions provided by the two rival hostesses.

The excitement generated by table croquet never vanished, and invitations to Mallards to play the game were very much sought after. Major Benjy, when not inspired by wine, proved to be a competent and occasionally skilful player, part of which may have been the result of his golfing experience. When he was partnered with Mr Wyse, the two of them were unbeatable.

Despite entreaties by Georgie and others to do so, Lucia refused to play the game for money, though on the occasions that she did not play, but merely took the part of a spectator, she permitted her guests (and Georgie) to play for modest stakes.

"This is excellent practice for the summer," Georgie told Lucia. "When we can go outside and play on the lawn again, I shall know exactly what to do."

"And so will our guests. I think we might even start the Tilling Croquet Association, don't you?"

"With you as President?" said Georgie.

"I hardly think that I would be worthy of such an honour. Perhaps Mr Wyse should be Honorary President, given his past experience of the game. But upon consideration, I believe it would make most sense for either you or me to be one of the officers of the Club, perhaps as Secretary, since most of our games will be held here. Diva's lawn at Wasters is far too small to be considered, and I do not think that the Wyses, even if Mr Wyse should become President, have the correct shape of lawn for croquet. The Vicarage lawn, as I recall, seems to be given over to the moles for their benefit. There is Grebe, of course, where if you will remember, I laid down an excellent lawn, if it has not been swept away in the last floods.

TWENTY-EIGHT

However, it is a little far out of town for a game of croquet."

"You are being perfectly ridiculous," Georgie said. "You know this is the only house in town where there could be regular games of croquet. We have room for at least two, possibly three, courts here. There is nowhere else. And as for me being Secretary, well, I don't think that's a very good idea, is it? You are the one with all the—" Georgie was going to say "push", but thought better of it at the last minute "—skills, and can get things done so much better than I could."

"Too kind, my dear. Very well, if you insist, I will talk to Mr Wyse and ask him to become the President of the Tilling Croquet Club, making it clear to him that it will involve him in no extra work, since that will be carried out by the Secretary. You will join him and me on the Committee, I hope?"

"If you think I will be useful."

"Not just useful, Georgie. You will be essential."

"Oh, very well then. And Elizabeth, will she be a member?"

"*Chi sa?* Who knows? If she wishes to join together with her husband, who are we to prevent her? However, I do not consider that her temperament is altogether suited to the game."

TWENTY-NINE

At Grebe, Elizabeth continued to exclude Lucia from all gatherings of mah-jong, on the grounds that it might cause needless embarrassment. The fact that the same courtesy had been extended by Lucia to Elizabeth was also a factor in her calculations.

Mah-jong continued to be a popular diversion in Tilling, and the Padre, for one, found it a pleasant change from bridge. After many fiercely fought battles over the bridge tables, it would be a poor intellect indeed (a description which did not apply to any of the Tilling players) that failed to know the contents of her or his opponents' hands. The individual strategies of each player were by now far too well known

TWENTY-NINE

to be interesting, and the extremes of surprised joy when one's deductions were proved correct, and despair generated by one's failure to calculate accurately were now missing.

Added to which, bridge also involved the use of dummy, which meant that one player had to sit idly by, effectively deprived of partaking in the pleasant discussions provided by revokes and their subsequent denial, and other delights associated with the poor tactics of one's opponents (and one's partner). Mah-jong, on the other hand, allowed each player the pleasure of not just two, but three opponents whose play could be criticised, providing all players with an afternoon of constructive entertainment.

Against this, though, could be set Elizabeth's setting of herself up as judge, jury, and executioner when it became necessary to refer to the rules of the game. The Major's book, which had been so often in evidence when the games were first played, was now declared to be unnecessary by Elizabeth, who claimed to have memorised the contents.

Diva had been seen by Georgie ordering a copy of *Snyder's Ma-Jung Manual*, but a week later, she confessed to him that she found it hard to understand.

"You need the tiles in front of you to work

it out," she complained, "and the rules are too complicated. And the way that Elizabeth explains them – well, sometimes she seems to say one thing, and then the next time she says something completely different. I don't believe she really knows herself what she is doing. I've a good mind to say something to her about it."

"I agree," said Georgie. "I think she's making up the rules sometimes, and it makes it very difficult for any of us to win, I've found."

"Have you heard from Irene, by the way?" Diva asked him. "It's been a few weeks now since she went off to London."

"Not directly, but I did receive a letter from Olga the other day. She says that Mr Abramov has finished the final version of his opera, and that Irene has produced some beautiful designs for it." Olga had also mentioned, though Georgie refrained from telling Diva, that Sasha seemed to have adopted the memory of Diva as his muse, inspiring his music from afar.

"I wonder if we will ever get to see them," Diva said.

THIRTY

Their conversation was interrupted by a familiar voice hailing them from some way off. "Hello, you two! What a stroke of luck finding you together. I have something for you both."

"Irene!" said Georgie. "When did you arrive back from London?"

"Just now. And I must go back the day after tomorrow. But Olga insisted, and so did Sasha, that I should deliver these to you two personally."

She fished in the pocket of her men's overcoat, and produced two envelopes.

"And I simply *must* go and see Lucia soon," she said. "Oh, there's Elizabeth. No envelope for her, I'm afraid." She went down the street in the opposite direction to Elizabeth and had soon turned the corner.

"Good morning, dear Diva, and you Mr Georgie," Elizabeth beamed at them. "Was that quaint Irene I saw just now?"

"Yes, it was. She's here for a few days, she said. She must return to London the day after tomorrow."

"Oh yes, she's doing something with the theatre, isn't she?" Elizabeth pretended to think. "Oh yes, with your admirer, Diva. That Russian."

Diva's face turned bright red with suppressed fury, and it looked as though she was going to say something very unpleasant indeed to Elizabeth, but Georgie intervened.

"Yes, that's right," he said. "She's designing the scenery and the costumes at Covent Garden."

"Well, that will be nice for Covent Garden, won't it? A little bit of quaintness will do them no harm, I would think."

"Quite," said Georgie. He wasn't going to allow himself to say more.

"Anyway, you'll both come tomorrow afternoon to play mah-jong, won't you?"

"Thank you very much," said Georgie. "Half-past two?"

THIRTY

"That's right. And you, Diva dear?"

"Can't," Diva said firmly. "Dentist."

"Oh, very well then. Maybe I could call at Taormina and see if Irene would like to come."

"Would you take it amiss if I were to save you the trouble and issue the invitation on your behalf?" Georgie asked.

"That would be most kind," Elizabeth said. "Thank you so much. *Au reservoir*."

"Do you really have to go to the dentist tomorrow?" Georgie asked Diva when Elizabeth was out of sight.

"Don't now, but I will have to go tomorrow. It would be just like Elizabeth to go checking up. I'm not going there to be made fun of and insulted by her. And she cheats with the rules. I'm sure of it."

"What's in the envelopes, I wonder?" Georgie said, hoping to change the subject.

"Shall we see?" said Diva. "Come on, let's open them together in my house." She led the way into her front room. "Oh look!" she exclaimed, tearing open her envelope and extracting the card inside. "It's an invitation to the *première* of the opera in London! A box in Covent Garden! How exciting!"

Georgie had opened his envelope by now, more carefully. "And Lucia and me, too," he said. "How kind of Olga. The three of us can travel together, see the opera, maybe meet Olga afterwards, spend the night in an hotel, and come back together."

"Oh what fun!" said Diva. "Now I shall lie awake wondering what to wear."

"So shall I," said Georgie. "But I must be off. I must give that invitation to Irene, and then give the good news to Lucia."

"And I am sure there is no invitation for Elizabeth and her Benjy-boy," said Diva.

"Now, now, we mustn't gloat," said Georgie. But he was still smiling as he knocked on the door of Taormina.

"Georgie-porgie, conqueror of my heart, how perfectly delightful to see you. Will you come in?"

"Oh, no, no." Irene's attentions always made Georgie feel flustered. "Thank you so much for the invitations."

"Not me, my dear sweet Georgie. You must thank Olga and Sasha. They are perfect pets to work with, and when this monster of an opera is all over and down with, I must tell you all about them. It has been a perfect joy to escape the Tilling philistines, I can tell you, and to have my genius appreciated by all and sundry."

"And," Georgie added, "Elizabeth has invited

THIRTY

you to Grebe tomorrow afternoon at half-past two. I'm invited too, so Cadman can drive us there together and fetch us back."

"No Lucia?"

"No, it's to play mah-jong, you see. And you need four people to play. Have you ever played?"

"I think I might be able to manage. So, you and I against the massed might of the Mapp-Flints, eh?"

"Quite so. Come to Mallards at two and we'll motor down together. Now I must go and tell Lucia the good news about the opera."

"I'll come with you," said Irene.

THIRTY-ONE

Lucia received the news of the invitation to the opera with what might be termed 'modified rapture'.

"I dare say that Mr Abramov will have produced something that does dear Olga's voice justice. There are some lovely notes there, I confess, though when dear Pepino and I saw the *première* of *Lucrezia* all those years ago, Signor Cortese did not do her voice justice. But then, I suppose I am too critical. And dear Diva will accompany us? How delightful. I was not aware that she was such a devotee of opera." She paused, and turned to Irene. "And now you are to take a turn at Elizabeth's latest passion? This Chinese thing?"

Thirty-one

"I have been invited, and it might pass a wet afternoon. Even if the game is not exciting, I can always use the time making sketches for my next painting."

"How nice, dear. What is it to be called?"

"'A vision of Hell' in the style of a Hieronymus Bosch, as my 'Birth of Venus' was in the style of Botticelli."

"And will we be in it?" asked Georgie.

"Only the select few will see themselves there," said Irene. "And it is I who will be doing the selecting. Now, Lucia, no-one tells me anything. Mapp has her mah-jong. What have you got?"

"I do not know what you mean."

"Oh, Lucia, you know that it is a universal law of nature. If you have something, Mapp must have her own something in competition, and *vice versa*. It's one of Newton's laws, or if it isn't, then it should have been. So come on, out with it, what have you got?"

"We've been playing croquet," Georgie told her.

"In this weather?" Irene put a finger to her head and twirled it in a vulgar gesture.

"Indoors," Georgie added. "Come and see."

He led the way to the garden-room where the croquet court was still set out on the table.

142 – A Tilling New Year

"Oh, what fun!" Irene exclaimed as she grasped the idea. "Whoever would have thought of something like that?"

Georgie coughed in a way that he hoped was modest. Irene looked at him.

"I do believe it was you, Georgie! Why, you're blushing. Genius, my dear sweet little Georgie-porgie, sheer genius. When we come back from Mapp's, can we have a game together?"

"Why not? That is, if we're still in a good mood after visiting Mapp."

"I'm sure we will be."

THIRTY-TWO

Georgie had Cadman drive Irene and himself to Grebe, and they were ushered into the drawing-room, where the card-table was already set out.

Elizabeth patiently explained the rules to Irene, who followed her instructions silently, though a keen observer, such as Georgie, might have noticed a faint upward tugging at the corners of her mouth as some of Elizabeth's explanations were being given.

The first game was won easily by Irene.

"You *have* picked it up quickly, dear one," said Elizabeth, smiling through clenched teeth. "I had hardly started to collect my sweet little winds. Let us play again."

This time it was Elizabeth who claimed victory, calling "Mah-jong" and displaying her hand for inspection.

"That's not a winning hand," said Irene, bluntly.

"Dear one, look. Three eights of circles, and three sevens of bamboo. A two, three, four of bamboos, East, West and North winds, and a pair of red dragons. Four sets of three and a pair."

"Can't have three different winds as one of the sets."

"I'm sure you can," said Elizabeth. "It's in the rule book."

"Can't. Tell you what," said Irene. "How much money will you win off us all if you do win?"

"Two shillings, I believe."

"Then I'll make a deal with you. If that rule about the winds is in the book, then I will pay you, not two shillings, but two pounds. But if you can't find that rule, then you pay me two pounds. Deal?"

Elizabeth sat back, a stricken expression on her face. "I... I may be mistaken. As you wish, quaint one. Let us not bother with the book. I am sure you are right."

"In that case, I believe you owe us all

Hugh Ashton – 145

eightpence, as the penalty for declaring before you were ready."

Elizabeth swept the tiles together so furiously preparatory to building the next wall that several of them dropped to the floor and Georgie and the Major spent some time retrieving them.

Irene won that next game as well.

Never, in all her reign as queen of mah-jong had Elizabeth been humiliated so thoroughly as that afternoon. Not only did Irene win every game with an ease that seemed positively indecent, but she challenged her hostess' rulings on the conduct of play in such a way that Elizabeth was forced to back down every time.

"Your winnings, dear one," said Elizabeth at the end of the afternoon. "Eighteen shillings and tuppence."

"Oh, forget the tuppence," said Irene. "Eighteen shillings will be jolly useful. And that's nine and a penny from you, Major Benjy, and the same from you, Georgie." She pocketed her winnings with satisfaction. "Heigh-ho, Georgie, time for home."

In the car, Georgie turned to Irene. "I am sure you have played before. I confess I did enjoy watching Elizabeth's face when you threatened to look up that rule in the book."

Irene laughed. "Played before? I should say I have. My dear Georgie, for two years of my life, I did nothing but play mah-jong with my fellow students. That is, when I wasn't painting. And I was good at it, too. Paid for many a bottle of wine with my mah-jong."

"Are we going to let the others know what happened?"

"I don't see why not. If Mapp's been cheating them all these past weeks, they deserve to know what she's been up to, don't you think?"

"I suppose so."

"Anyway, I can't wait to tell Lucia. And then that nice game of croquet you promised me. And I promise you that I've only played croquet twice in my life, and never on a table, so I'm trusting you not to do what Mapp does and make up the rules as you go."

"I would never—" said Georgie.

"I know you wouldn't, my dear. You're far too much of a dear old lady ever to do such a thing, and that's why I am so fond of you."

THIRTY-THREE

Lucia's reaction, when Irene had told her about her and Georgie's mah-jong game, was one of lofty indifference.

"Since I have never played the game against her," she said, "there is no reason for me to despise her."

"But she cheated and lied to everyone," protested Irene. "You must feel something."

"I feel sad," Lucia pronounced from a great moral height. "Sad that she feels she has to have these petty triumphs based on deception. If I were Major Benjy—"

"—you wouldn't be so silly as to put yourself in that position," said Irene, "and even if you were, you would never have let her carry on like that."

"I was going to say," Lucia said mildly, "that if I were Major Benjy, I should be searching for a good nerve doctor for poor Elizabeth."

This was clearly to be Lucia's line, and neither Georgie nor Irene could divert her from it.

It took very little time, thanks to Irene, for the news of the challenge to Elizabeth's perfidy, and her ultimate capitulation, to spread throughout Tilling.

"I knew it," said Diva to Georgie, having been informed of the previous day's doings by the Padre. "I told you so, didn't I?"

"I have to confess I suspected her as well," said Georgie. "But the trouble was that none of us knew the rules of the game well enough to be able to challenge her when we felt she was going wrong."

"And to think of all the money I lost to her playing that stupid game," said Diva. "I've half a mind to march down to Grebe and shout at her and Benjy until I get it all back."

"How much have you lost?" asked Georgie. "If you don't mind saying, that is."

"Two shillings and ninepence," said Diva stiffly. "Quite enough to be making a fuss over, if you ask me."

THIRTY-THREE

"Oh, definitely," said Georgie. "But you might wait until she repays out of the goodness of her heart."

"Ho!" Diva retorted. "I'd be waiting until the sky is full of flying pigs, wouldn't I?"

The Padre and Evie, who had been the first to whom Irene had communicated the news, were at that moment talking to Susan Wyse.

"And then Irene told us that she had been playing mah-jong since she was at the College of Art, and she knew the rules inside out, so there was no way that Elizabeth could have won," Evie squeaked in excitement.

"Aye, 'tis a sair thing for me to mind that I have one of my own kirk exposed in this way," said the Padre solemnly.

"But this is monstrous!" said Susan. "I cannot believe that anyone could be so wicked." Her husband, who had been busy with some purchases in the stationer's, joined them, and bowed to the Padre and Evie.

"Algernon, Evie has just been telling me some things about Elizabeth Mapp-Flint which have shocked me to my core," his wife told him.

"Indeed?"

Evie explained what she had been told by Irene, and Mr Wyse shook his head sadly. "It did appear to me," he admitted, "that at times

Mrs Mapp-Flint's explanations of the game seemed to contradict each other, but I had put that down to my own failings in the fields of memory and general understanding."

"But what are we to do, Algernon?"

It was the Padre who answered. "As a minister of the kirk, I canna continue to play that heathen game with Mistress Mapp-Flint. Until she confesses her misdeeds, that is."

"Thank you, Padre. I believe that is the correct path for us all to follow. Let us hope that the poor misguided woman will see the error of her ways before long."

Diva came bustling up following her conversation with Georgie. "What are we to do?" she asked. There was no need for her to elaborate further – everyone had only one topic of conversation.

"We are going to refuse all of Elizabeth's invitations," Susan told her.

"That is, until she apologises and promises to behave," she added.

"And what about the money that she won from us?" asked Diva.

There was a silence, broken by Mr Wyse. "If I may be permitted to make a suggestion," he said, "that is a sleeping dog that I am happy to leave lying asleep, if you will excuse the

Thirty-Three

metaphor. It is my opinion that such an action might well cause more troubles than it would solve."

There was a murmur of general agreement.

"Oh, very well," said Diva. "It would look wrong if it was only me asking for my winnings to be returned. Not that I shall forget about it, of course."

THIRTY-FOUR

"Of all the—" exclaimed Elizabeth furiously, crumpling up the note that had just been delivered, and hurling it with some force into the fireplace.

"What is it, Liz?"

"The Wyses. Algernon and Susan. They regret that their time is otherwise engaged and therefore cannot come to play mah-jong."

"That's all of them, then?" asked the Major.

"Yes, that's all of them, thanks to Irene. I had hoped that Mr Wyse would be a gentleman. I had no great expectations of the Padre, or even Mr Georgie for that matter, but for the Wyses to refuse..." She sank into a sulky silence.

"What's in the other envelope?"

"Nothing of interest," she said, tossing it towards the fireplace. It was just possible to read the words 'Mallards House' printed at the top of the blue laid writing paper. The Major knew better than to enquire further as to the contents.

"And if you will do the marketing this morning, Benjy-boy," Elizabeth said in a wheedling tone, "I should be most grateful. My headache is back again, and I really do not feel that I could manage to go there and back today. I will make a list for you."

"Very good," said the Major, though he was perceptive enough to realise that he would be widely viewed as at least an accessary before and after the fact to his wife's behaviour. It would be some time, he feared, before he could enjoy a quiet whisky and soda in the Club.

EPILOGUE

It was a few weeks afterwards that Lucia gave a dinner-party, following the visit to London by Georgie, Diva and herself to the triumphant *première* of *Tsarina Ekaterina*.

Alas, dear Olga could not be present, and neither could Sasha, who were both busy performing the opera, which had been hailed as a work of the highest quality in the national press. However, the designer of the scenery and costumes, Miss Irene Coles, had accepted her invitation, and her work had also been lauded in the newspapers for its boldness and originality, mixing, as one critic put it, "Muscovite barbarity with European classical sensitivity".

There had been some discussion between

EPILOGUE

Georgie and Lucia as to whether to invite Elizabeth and Major Benjy.

"After what she has done," said Georgie, "I am not sure that anyone else would be happy to meet her. Diva especially feels the loss of her two shillings and ninepence."

"Dear Diva," said Lucia. "Always so careful with her pennies. But she must come. Irene apparently has something important to give her."

"How exciting. What is it?"

"She won't tell me."

"Tarsome. I've never known Irene to keep a secret before now."

"She says it's a present from Mr Abramov."

"Oh dear. I hope it's not too embarrassing for Diva. I remember that New Year's Eve party at Grebe."

"Irene says it's not too embarrassing."

"But then she has rather different standards of what is embarrassing and what is not," said Georgie. "But if it's a gift, I suppose it must be given."

"And what better occasion to give it than at a dinner party where we're all friends together? I shall invite Elizabeth and Benjy. He can sit next to me, and I will put Elizabeth between Mr Wyse and you at the other end of the table."

"Lobster *à la Riseholme*?" asked Georgie.

"No, I think Elizabeth would see that as needless provocation. In any event, lobsters are not at their best at this time of year. I think it will be sole *bonne femme*. And then for the main course, a nice sirloin of beef."

The dinner party assembled. The first to arrive was Irene, who for the first time in anyone's memory was wearing a skirt, albeit with a man's corduroy shirt and tweed jacket. As she entered the room, Georgie, who had been deputed by Lucia to greet the guests with sherry, raised a questioning eyebrow as he glanced downwards.

"It was one of Olga's. What she called her 'sensible country skirt'," she explained. "She said I should sometimes try to let the world know that I have legs, which I thought was a rather silly comment for her to make, because what am I walking on if I don't have legs, but there you are. So I'm wearing it."

"And very nice you look in it too," said Georgie.

"Sherry?" asked Irene, changing the subject, and Georgie handed her a glass. "Is Mapp going to be here tonight?"

"Yes, but you're not going to be sitting anywhere near her," Georgie reassured her.

"Good. One of us might say something that

could lead to a breach of the peace. *Quai hai*, as Major Benjy would say," as she raised her glass in salute. "To Mallards, and all who sail in her."

The garden-room gradually filled with the Tillingites. Diva came over to join Irene and Georgie.

"I really did enjoy the opera," she said to Irene. "And it was so nice for us all to go to supper afterwards with you and Miss Bracely and Mr Abramov."

"Wouldn't you like an outfit like Ekaterina's in the last act, Mrs Plaistow?"

"Oh dear, no. All that gold and brocade. Were those costumes very heavy, Irene? I felt sorry for Miss Bracely having to sing while she was wearing them."

"Oh no. The crown and jewels were mostly cardboard and *papier mâché* and the brocade was very lightweight."

"I am glad of that. And how nicely Mr Abramov behaved himself, didn't he? It was a pleasure to talk with him after his behaviour at that New Year party."

"You're lucky that you weren't hugged by him," said Irene. "He's like a great hairy smelly bear. He tried to kiss me once, but I told him I wasn't going to have any of that. Anyway, he gave me a gift to you from him, which I shall present to you after dinner," Irene told her.

"Oh, that does sound exciting," Diva said.

"A veritable triumph, Miss Coles," Mr Wyse said, joining the little group. "All accounts in the newspapers are full of praise for you. Susan and I will definitely be paying a visit to Covent Garden when we next go up to Town."

"Thank you, Mr Wyse." It was clear that Olga, as well as giving a skirt to Irene, had also bestowed on her some social graces, qualities which even her most fervent admirers would admit were sadly lacking at times.

However, any hopes that Irene would no longer merit the epithet 'quaint' were dashed when Elizabeth and Major Mapp-Flint entered the room. "Oh look, it's the Green Dragon and the North Wind," exclaimed Irene in a clear voice that carried across the room. Indeed, Elizabeth was wearing a green dress, and her husband was dressed in the same outfit in which he had been portrayed as the North Wind in Irene's famous Picture of the Year, her 'Birth of Venus'.

A look of pure fury appeared on Elizabeth's face as Georgie choked on his sherry, Diva smirked, and even Mr Wyse could be observed attempting to keep a serious expression.

Hugh Ashton – 159

EPILOGUE

"Sherry, dear Elizabeth?" asked Lucia soothingly, and all who heard remembered that time at the house-warming, when Elizabeth, in a self-proclaimed delicate condition (subsequently dismissed eloquently by Lucia as a "wind-egg"), had proclaimed it to be poison.

In this instance, however, she accepted with alacrity, as did her husband, and Georgie hastened to fill two glasses which he brought over to the Mapp-Flints, thinking it best that they keep a physical distance from Irene.

As the Padre and Evie arrived, all the guests were now assembled, and were summoned to dinner by Grosvenor's beating of the gong.

The sole was much appreciated by all, and on Elizabeth's asking whether she could have the recipe, Lucia promised to send it to her the next day.

The subjects of mah-jong and croquet were tactfully avoided by all, including Irene, and Mr Wyse skilfully steered the conversation in the general direction of bridge. This was a subject in which all participants considered themselves to be expert, and all bones of contention had been thoroughly chewed and all flesh stripped off them until there was almost nothing left in the way of contentious matter.

A pleasant time was then spent by all arguing

the advantages of majority calling over psychic bidding, and the other schools of thought which went to make up the Tilling bridge world. However, all attempts to convert the adherent of one religion to another fell on the stony ground of fanatical dogmatism. Nonetheless, it was felt by all that Mr Wyse had performed a valuable service in his setting a course away from croquet and mah-jong.

Following dessert (a trifle based on a compote based around bottled apricots), Georgie rapped on his glass with his spoon and called for silence.

"Our guest who has distinguished herself in London, and covered herself with glory as she has covered Miss Olga Bracely with a magnificent costume, and the stage of Covent Garden with scenery, Miss Irene Coles, would like to say a few words."

A rather embarrassed Irene rose to her feet. "That was very elegant, Georgie. Thank you. I have a message from Sasha Abramov to you, Diva."

"Me?" Diva appeared astonished.

"Yes, you. And a gift, as I told you earlier. Let me read what he has to say to you." Irene removed a paper from the inside of her jacket. "'Alas, I came to realise that I could never be

EPILOGUE

yours and you could never be mine, my dear Mrs Plaistow. But the sight of your face, which reminded me so of my darling Ludmilla, has inspired me to produce what I believe to be my masterpiece. My dear Muse, please accept this with my sincere gratitude. Yours, Alexander Davidovich Abramov'." Irene reached under the table and held up a large envelope.

While this message was being read, Diva turned a shade of beetroot red with embarrassment.

"Aye well, and ye're an inspiration to us all," called out the Padre.

There was a round of applause in which it was noticed by Georgie, at least, that Elizabeth did not join as Diva struggled to her feet and accepted the envelope from Irene.

"Dear Mrs Plaistow, you are too cruel. Pray enlighten us as to the contents," Mr Wyse begged her.

"Wait a moment, my hands are sticky," said Diva. She wiped her hands carefully on her napkin, and then opened the envelope to draw out a large piece of paper.

"It's the title page of the manuscript of *Tsarina Ekaterina*," explained Irene.

"And such a kind inscription," said Diva. "'To my Muse, Mrs Plaistow, whom I will always remember with affection and gratitude.' And then his signature."

While this presentation had been proceeding, Elizabeth's face had been setting in a grim mask. The disastrous incident that had ruined her New Year party had somehow turned into a triumph – but a triumph for another, not her. "How nice for you, dear Diva," she positively snarled. "You will have to ask Janet to put it where everyone will see it, like dear Susan's MBE, which her servants seem always to leave lying about."

"I don't think Janet would do anything like that," Diva retorted. "I shall have it framed, and hang it in place of one of your watercolours that I have hanging in my sitting-room."

Elizabeth seemed to be girding her loins for a counter-attack, and Susan appeared ready to enter the fray on Diva's side to counter Elizabeth's accusations but Lucia, in her role as the League of Nations, stepped in to prevent further bloodshed in the threatened tripartite war.

"How generous of Mr Abramov to give you that, dear Diva, and I am sure that you will find a suitable place for it without disturbing all the sweet little pickies you have already. Now, everybody, if we all move into the garden-room,

I am sure that Grosvenor has set out two tables for bridge. There are ten of us, so Georgie and I will sit out for the first rubber."

"Dear Lucia, how noble and unselfish of you," said Elizabeth. "But it will not be necessary. Benjy-boy and I must leave you now. We have another appointment which it is impossible to miss."

"Eh? What?"

"You *must* remember," Elizabeth cooed in velvety tones, but it was a velvet that covered a will of steel.

"Oh yes. How stupid of me. Nearly forgot." The Major wiped his moustache, muttering something that even Lucia's sharp ears were unable to distinguish, and rose to his feet.

Thanking their hostess, and bidding farewell to all, the Mapp-Flints made their way out of the house. No one bothered to see in which direction they had departed – it was clear that their destination would be Grebe.

"The puir mannie," said the Padre. "He will be missing his wee dram, I ween."

Bridge beckoned. All were drawn to the two tables. Despite the lack of Elizabeth as an opponent and a partner, thereby depriving them all of the chance of a potential pleasant altercation, welcome pockets of dispute soon sprang up, even on the table where Mr Wyse was playing, and a comforting familiarity soon spread over the assembled company as the cards were played, and pennies (and on Susan Wyse's table sixpences) changed hands.

If you enjoyed this story...

Please consider writing a review on a Web site such as Amazon or Goodreads.

You may also enjoy some adventures of Sherlock Holmes by Hugh Ashton, who has been described in *The District Messenger*, the newsletter of the Sherlock Holmes Society of London, as being "one of the best writers of new Sherlock Holmes stories, in both plotting and style".

Volumes published so far include :

Tales from the Deed Box of John H. Watson M.D.
More from the Deed Box of John H. Watson M.D.
Secrets from the Deed Box of John H. Watson M.D.
The Darlington Substitution (novel)
Notes from the Dispatch-Box of John H. Watson M.D.
Further Notes from the Dispatch-box of John H. Watson M.D.
The Death of Cardinal Tosca (novel)
The Last Notes from the Dispatch-box of John H. Watson, M.D.
The Trepoff Murder (ebook only)
1894
Without my Boswell

If you enjoyed this story...

Some Singular Cases of Mr. Sherlock Holmes
The Lichfield Murder
The Adventure of the Bloody Steps
The Adventure of Vanaprastha (ebook only)

Children's detective stories, with beautiful illustrations by Andy Boerger, the first of which was nominated for the prestigious Caldecott Prize :

Sherlock Ferret and the Missing Necklace
Sherlock Ferret and The Multiplying Masterpieces
Sherlock Ferret and The Poisoned Pond
Sherlock Ferret and the Phantom Photographer
The Adventures of Sherlock Ferret

Short stories, thrillers, alternative history, and historical science fiction titles:

Tales of Old Japanese
At the Sharpe End
Balance of Powers
Beneath Gray Skies
Red Wheels Turning
Angels Unawares
The Untime
The Untime Revisited
Unknown Quantities
Mapp at Fifty
Mapp's Return
La Lucia

Full details of all of these and more at : https://HughAshtonBooks.com

ABOUT THE AUTHOR

Hugh Ashton was born in the United Kingdom, and moved to Japan in 1988, where he lived until his return to the UK in 2016.

He is best known for his Sherlock Holmes stories, which have been hailed as some of the most authentic pastiches on the market, and have received favourable reviews from Sherlockians and non-Sherlockians alike.

He has also published other work in a number of genres, including alternative history, historical science fiction, and thrillers, based in Japan, the USA, and the UK.

He currently lives in the historic city of Lichfield with his wife, Yoshiko.

His ramblings may be found on Facebook, Twitter, and in various other places on the Internet. He may be contacted at: author@HughAshtonBooks.com